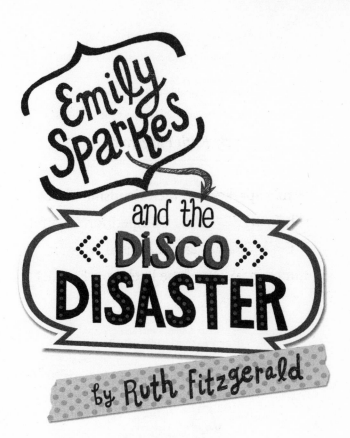

Emily Sparkes
and the
«« Disco »»
DISASTER

by Ruth Fitzgerald

LITTLE, BROWN BOOKS FOR YOUNG READERS
www.lbkids.co.uk

LITTLE, BROWN BOOKS FOR YOUNG READERS

First published in Great Britain in 2016 by Hodder & Stoughton

Text copyright © 2016 by Ruth Fitzgerald
Illustrations copyright © 2016 by Allison Cole

The moral rights of the author and illustrator have been asserted.

A CIP catalogue record for this book
is available from the British Library.

ISBN 978-0-34900-187-6

Typeset in Minion by M Rules
Printed and bound in Great Britain by
Clays Ltd, St Ives plc

The paper and board used in this book are made from
wood from responsible sources.

MIX
Paper from
responsible sources
FSC® C104740

Little, Brown Books for Young Readers
An imprint of Hachette Children's Group
Part of Hodder & Stoughton
Carmelite House
50 Victoria Embankment
London EC4Y 0DZ

An Hachette UK Company
www.hachette.co.uk

www.hachettechildrens.co.uk

"I have read the first Emily Sparkes book and really LOVE it … it's lots of fun and a really cool read!" Cathy Cassidy, bestselling author of The Chocolate Box Girls series

"Utterly hilarious and utterly relatable, Ruth Fitzgerald just gets all of the awful problems associated with being eleven years old. Everything in Emily Sparkes's life is a crisis, and each crisis is funnier than the last. Bring on the next book!" Robin Stevens, author of *Murder Most Unladylike* (Wells and Wong Mysteries)

"I laughed and laughed at *Emily Sparkes and the Friendship Fiasco*! She's like a younger Georgia Nicolson." Susie Day, author of *Pea's Book of Best Friends* (Pea's Book series)

"Lots to appeal to fans of Cathy Cassidy and Dork Diaries in this funny new series" *Bookseller*

"Once you start reading this book you won't be able to put it down. It's true to life and very funny. Emily Sparkes is everyone's dream best friend!" Alice, 12

"I thought this was side-splittingly funny and very realistic. Emily Sparkes is someone I'd want to be friends with!" Sterrett, 10

"Emily Sparkes is my new favourite character. She made me laugh a lot!" Piper, 11

"Emily Sparkes is amazingly funny." Maddie, 12

For more fab reviews visit www.ruthfitzgerald.co.uk

By Ruth Fitzgerald

Emily Sparkes and the Friendship Fiasco
Emily Sparkes and the Competition Calamity
Emily Sparkes and the Disco Disaster
Emily Sparkes and the Backstage Blunder

CONTENTS

To Laura – you're going to need bookshelves!

CHAPTER 1

Megatronic Mayhem

Wednesday evening

"*Yeah, baby, love you baby,*
   Yeah, baby, love you baby,
   Yeah, baby, laser love,
   Yeah, baby,
   Yeeeeah!"

Seriously, these are supposed to be the words to a *song*. If I was a songwriter and that was the best I could come up with, I'd hastily retrain as a bricklayer or something. Someone must have thought the lyrics were good, though, because they are printed out on the back of this ancient LP of my dad's.

If you don't know what an LP is, don't worry, because that means you are a modern person and not from the olden days. Basically, it is like a CD but more rubbish.

My dad was supposed to be getting a box of books down from the attic for Mum, before she got back from Tesco, but instead he found an old record player. He has spent half the evening trying to get it to work and, unfortunately, he has now succeeded and is forcing me to listen to all his crusty, crackly old records.

"I'm going to have to play it again, Emily," he says. "'Laser Love' by The Megatronics – they were *great*." He starts the track again: a scratchy,

squawky rock star yelling, "Yeah, baby!" to a screeching guitar.

I am thinking, *It is very lucky for Dad that Mum has gone to Tesco because she would be screeching even louder than The Megatronics if she had to listen to this racket.*

"Just listen to that guitar solo," Dad says, jumping up to play an invisible guitar and wave his equally invisible hair about.

"I don't have much choice, do I?" I say. Well, shout, actually.

I wouldn't mind so much but I am trying to concentrate on what is happening next door. The house next door has been empty for about three months, since Mrs Theodopolis went into the Silver Years Retirement Home. But it looks like someone might be moving in. I can only see a bit of what is going on because the hedge is in the way, but there is definitely a big white van outside.

There is also a brown sofa, which is either floating through the air just above the hedge or being carried by someone I can't see.

I am just wondering if I should go and try to get a better view from upstairs when my ancient phone makes a horrible bleeping sound, which is its way of telling me I have a message.

Have you seen the school newsletter?

Zuzanna, my second-best friend and the sort of person who reads school newsletters.

I go and dig out the newsletter from the bottom of my bag. There are four things on it:

1. *We raised £419.23 for Children in Need by having a "Wear Spotty Clothes to School" day. This is a marvellous result for such a small school as Juniper Road. Congratulations to everyone who took part!*

(I thought this was very unimaginative. There was a school on TV who made their head teacher abseil down the side of a twenty-storey building, but Mr Meakin felt that would interfere too much with the school day.)

2. *If anyone has found a stripy scarf, last seen in the dinner hall, would they please return it to Mr Meakin?*
3. *Allotment Club will restart after half-term.*
4. *The school fete will go ahead Wednesday 29th, 2.30 p.m. to 4.30 p.m. All welcome.*

I cannot at all think which one of these thrilling pieces of information has got Zuzanna so worked up she couldn't wait till tomorrow to tell me. It definitely can't be Children in Need day: she still hasn't really got over her mum coming in to school to help, wearing a pink leopard-print onesie. Also, my mum's Allotment Club is something we try to avoid mentioning.

I message back:

I don't see anything.

"This has got to be the best track ever!" Dad says. He has now stopped playing the invisible guitar and is playing the kitchen mop instead, standing on the sofa, bouncing his head up and down like a bald woodpecker. It is a very disturbing vision and it is lucky I am eleven and not at an impressionable age.

Fortunately, my phone beeps again and distracts me.

The PTA – no school disco – number 5!!!!

Number 5? What is she ...? Oh, hang on, there's more on the back. I turn the newsletter over and read:

5. *Due to lack of funds, it may not be possible to run the school half-term disco this year. An emergency meeting of the Parent Teachers' Association (PTA) will be held this Friday evening to discuss possible fund-raising activities. New members warmly welcomed.*

Oh no! School discos are the best fun. Not only do you get to go and have a laugh with your friends and listen to good music from DJ Derek Diamond's Disco ... (Get that, Dad? *Good* music. Like the NV Boyz – not The Mega-whatevers) ... but we get to see Mr Meakin in his cool, down-with-the-kids jeans which he thinks make him look really fashionable. (As if. Not even

if Cinderella's fairy godmother teamed up with
Gok Wan could that happen.)

My phone beeps again. Zuzanna is getting
impatient.

I've got a new dress and everything.

I reply:

I know. You told me!

About seven times, actually, I think.
Zuzanna messages back:

They need more PTA members to raise funds.

I text back:

What about your mum?

Zuzanna's mum loves that sort of thing. She's
basically a professional volunteer.

My mum is already on the PTA.

What about YOUR mum?

At that moment the door bursts open and Mum comes in with my baby sister, Clover, under one arm, and a big bag of shopping in her other hand. Clover is squawking almost as loudly as The Megatronics and Mum is looking like she lost her patience somewhere in Tesco's car park and definitely hasn't found it since.

She stares at Dad doing his rock star impression and then dumps the shopping on the floor. I am a little bit worried she might dump Clover too, but luckily she doesn't. There is a sharp scratching sound as she stops the record.

"Wha—?" Dad says, stopping mid head-bang. "Oh. Er ... hi! You're back early," he says, getting off the sofa with a nervous grin. "We were just listening to a bit of music."

"Music?" Mum snaps. "You do realise there are people moving in next door? You can hear this 'music' right down the street. What on earth must they think?"

Dad looks a bit sheepish and says, "Here, Emily, take this," thrusting the mop at me like it was my idea.

"I don't suppose you've got my books down, have you?" Mum says.

"Well ..." Dad starts.

"Thought not," Mum says, and she marches off to the kitchen shouting, "Completely irresponsible!"

Dad follows Mum into the kitchen and I can hear him saying, "Sorry, love. I'll go up to the attic now ..." but he is going to have to work a bit harder than that because she is already banging cupboard doors so loudly The Megatronics would probably give her an audition.

My phone bleeps:

Have u asked your mum?

I reply:

I will. Later.

Unfortunately, things don't get any better.

Half an hour later, Mum has calmed down enough to pop round to meet the new neighbours and offer them a cup of tea – and probably some earplugs. Dad is in the attic, hunting for Mum's books. I am about to start my homework but then I decide first I really need to rearrange all the books on my shelves in colour order. (If you have never done this you should – it looks fantastic.)

I have just got onto the yellows when the phone rings.

"Dad," I call up to the attic. "It's Uncle Clive on the phone."

"Er, OK. I'll come down," Dad calls back.

Uncle Clive is my dad's brother. He came to stay with us a little while ago and he was very nice, but I'm glad he made things up with his girlfriend, Daisy, and went back to live with her. He does have a way of taking up quite a lot of space.

"Hi, Uncle Clive. Dad won't be a minute. He's in the attic."

"Oh, ha! Is that where your mum's keeping him now?" he says, and then has a good chuckle at his own joke.

Dad comes down and takes the phone just as Mum comes back from seeing the new neighbours.

I am about to ask her if she has found out any

interesting facts, like do they have any kids and can they levitate sofas, but she is already frowning, listening to Dad on the phone.

"No, Clive, of course I haven't forgotten. Tomorrow? Er ... no problem. What's he called? Oh, right ... Got to go," Dad says as he spots Mum and he hangs up quickly. "Hello, love," he says.

"What's who called?" Mum says.

"Oh ... er ... no one, really. How are the neighbours?" Dad asks.

"They're a bit ... unusual," Mum says.

"Have they got any children?" I ask.

"Yes, there's a girl. About your age. She's ... interesting."

"Did they moan about Dad's music?" I ask.

"Not exactly – in fact, Griff, that's the man, said it was really good." She sighs. "Apparently he plays the guitar himself."

"Ha!" Dad laughs. "A man of taste."

"The lady seems nice – Wanda. She does yoga. She's going to teach me to meditate. It's good for stress," she says, looking at Dad. "You have got my books down, haven't you?"

"Almost," Dad says, rushing back towards the stairs. "Had to take a phone call ... from Clive."

"Clive? Oh, *no* – please don't tell me he wants to come back," Mum says. "I like Clive but I don't think I could live with him another day."

"No, Clive and Daisy are very happy. So much so that they're planning to go on holiday," Dad says, as he goes back up the stairs. He waits till he gets to the top then leans over the banister and calls down: "Which is why I said we'd be fine to look after their dog for the week."

I cannot put the next bit of what Mum says because it is a totally unsuitable thing for a mother of two to be saying. Also, it is lucky that Clover is asleep otherwise her first words might be very difficult to explain.

CHAPTER 2

No Go Disco

 *Thursday*

"They cannot be serious!" Chloe says. "This school is just such a dump. When I was at Mag Hall we had a disco every month with famous DJs, like ... like ... someone famous and DJ-ish."

"It's only a cancelled disco," I say. "I mean, I know it's a pity but it's not the end of the world."

17

Zuzanna, Chloe and I are sitting on the ENDSHIP SEA (my favourite bench in the playground – long story). Zuzanna has just read out the newsletter again. She and Chloe are taking it very badly.

"But it's the only fun thing we ever get to do at this school," Chloe says. "Everything else is just like ... *lessons.*"

"To be fair, Chloe, that is what a school is for," Zuzanna says. "But, I agree, it's very disappointing. Especially as *some* people's parents work extremely hard for the school to make sure this kind of thing can go ahead" – she looks right at me – "and other people's parents don't even bother to join the PTA."

"How about your mum, Chloe?" I say quickly. "Can't she do something?"

"My mum?" Chloe says. "No, she's *très* too busy with all her, er ... international travel."

18

"Her what?"

"Her new job. Travelling ... internationally."

"But what does she do?" asks Zuzanna.

"Mostly she catches aeroplanes and flies to places," Chloe says. "It's *totalement* important. Definitely more important than school stuff."

"Why do you keep speaking French?"

"Oh, do I? I think I get it from my mum."

"But she's not French," I say.

"She so is! *Totalement*-ely," Chloe says. "She was born in Milan."

"Milan is in Italy," Zuzanna says.

Chloe rolls her eyes. "I *know* that. Her parents were on holiday, from France, where they lived, being, like, really French." She turns to look at me. "Anyway, what about your mum, Emily? Why doesn't she join this Pete Yay thing?"

"PTA," Zuzanna says.
"It means Parent-Teacher
Association."

"Exactly. And if Zuzanna's
mum and that Pete Yay bloke are in it, your mum
should join too, Emily. She doesn't even have a
job," Chloe says.

"She does have a job, but she's on maternity
leave. She's just had a baby."

"That was weeks ago," Chloe says. "You can't
have it as an excuse for ever."

"It's not an excuse! My mum is always at school,"
I say. "She runs the Allotment Club, doesn't she?
Single-handed."

I try to say this proudly, but it's not
easy.

"I don't see how that helps anyone
to have fun," Chloe says.

"Well, lots of other kids like it," I say, "although
I admit my mum is a bit of a lunatic lettuce lover."

"A what?" Zuzanna says.

"Or maybe a crazy carrot cruncher." I giggle.

Chloe frowns. "Emily, can you stop with the vegetables now? You know I don't like them."

"Sorry," I say, but then I just can't help myself muttering: "Or a fanatical fennel fancier," and I have to slap my hand over my mouth. But it doesn't stop me making a snorty sound.

"Emily!" Chloe says. "You are making me feel ill! Anyway, fennel is just totes showing off."

I suck my cheeks in. "Sorry."

"Sometimes you can be so immature," Zuzanna says. "You seem to have forgotten we are discussing a serious issue here."

"Yes," Chloe says, standing up as the bell goes for the end of break. "So, Emily. It seems like it's up to you, really. You need to get your mum to stop thinking about" – she does a little shudder – "*vegetables* and join the Pete Yay thing, or there will be no school disco, and it will be mostly *all your fault*."

When I get home, Mum is definitely not in the mood to be asked about the PTA. You can tell by the way she is frowning into the freezer. "I suppose everyone is going to want to have dinner again tonight?" she says.

I am not really sure how to answer the question except to say, "Well, yeah. *Duh*," which I don't think would be a good idea, so I don't say anything.

"I don't see why I'm the only person around here who cooks the dinner," she says, banging the freezer shut and opening the fridge. "It's not like someone else couldn't do it now and again. I wasn't specially born with a cooking gene."

And I think, *That's true.* "Shall I do it?" I say. "I like cooking."

"No, you'll make a mess," Mum says, sniffing at a pack of sausages.

"Where's Clover?" I ask, thinking I might get a better conversation out of my six-week-old sister.

"Asleep upstairs," she says. "Did you know last night she slept through the night for the first time?"

"Yes, Mum, you told me this morning. About ten times."

"It is just so wonderful when you finally get a night's sleep. Babies are very sweet, but they are a lot of work."

I think it is not very fair to blame Clover for not sleeping; after all, she has only had six weeks to practise. My gran has been practising for sixty-eight years and she's always saying, "I didn't sleep well last night."

Mum is scowling again. "And as if I haven't got enough to do, we now have to look after this dog."

Mum finally gave in and agreed to look after the dog after I begged her all last night not to phone

Uncle Clive and say we couldn't. I had to promise to look after it, feed it and take it for walks.

I have always wanted a pet but Mum is totally not into having animals in the house. She did once let me have a goldfish but it wasn't much fun for taking on a walk, and it's also very easy to forget to feed something if it doesn't bark. At least we don't have to look after Lemmy, Uncle Clive's pet rat. Apparently he's being looked after by a friend. I really like Lemmy but last time he came he escaped and I spent about a week trying to catch him again.

"What sort of dog is it?" I ask.

"I have no idea. Your father" – you can tell Mum's in a bad mood when she calls Dad "your father" – "forgot to ask. Completely irresponsible, as usual," she says, banging the fridge door shut and making the bottles inside rattle. "All I know is that it's called Sabre."

"Sabre?" I say. "Oh, right." Sabre doesn't sound like the sort of dog who

chases a ball and wags its tail. I hope I haven't made a big mistake. "Sounds a bit scary," I say, imagining a row of sharp teeth and yellowy, mean eyes.

"Exactly what I said. It doesn't sound at all like the sort of dog that should be in the house. But if you want to look after it ... "

"When are they bringing it over?"

"Any time—"

Ding dong!

"—now."

Mum sighs and goes to the front door. I tag along at a safe distance – I don't want to get knocked flying by a great, big, growly dog.

Mum opens the door and Uncle Clive stands there with his enormous boots and his gappy-toothed smile. "'Ello, all. Thanks so much for looking after Sabre for us. You're a diamond," he says to Mum, as he walks into the hall.

"I didn't even know you had a dog," Mum says.

"Yes, Daisy got it to keep her company when we … when I was away. I think she loves it more than me now," he says, with a sort of laugh that sounds like he's not sure if it's something to laugh about.

"But where is it?" Mum asks, looking behind him cautiously. "I thought you were bringing him over."

"Here," Uncle Clive says, holding out a small wicker basket. A tiny little face peeps out from under a blanket and then snuggles back down again. I'm sure it can't be a dog – it's more like a guinea pig.

Mum looks confused. "But where's Sabre?" she asks.

"This is Sabre," Uncle Clive says. "He's a Chorkie. They're only little. Say hello, Sabre."

Sabre peeps out from under the blanket again. He has big brown eyes and looks a bit frightened.

27

"Ohhhhh!" I say. "He's lovely."

"But I thought he was going to be big," Mum says.

"No, you can't have a big dog on a motorbike. Sabre's just the right size. I can zip him up in my jacket."

Even Mum has stopped being in a bad mood. She takes the basket into the living room and we all watch as Sabre sits up and looks about.

"He's no trouble," Uncle Clive says. "Just needs a bit of food and a short walk and, apart from that, you'll have no bother at all."

Sabre climbs out of his basket and pads over to Mum. He really is very cute, not much bigger than a kitten. He puts his paw on her foot and looks up at her with

his big, round eyes. She picks him up and he curls up in her lap.

"Awww. He'll be fine," Mum says, smiling. "I have to admit I wasn't really looking forward to having a dog, but he's so sweet."

"He's Daisy's pride and joy," Uncle Clive says. "It took me ages to persuade her to go away without him."

"He can stay as long as he wants," Mum says, smiling at the fluffy bundle on her lap.

CHAPTER 3

Dog Days

"The sooner that dog goes, the better," Mum says. She is making toast for breakfast in a very grouchy way.

Basically, Sabre whined all night.

"I can't believe the baby slept all night and now I have a dog keeping me awake, instead," Mum says. "And he weed on the carpet."

31

Sabre is sitting in the corner looking a bit glum.

"He was probably missing being at home," I say.

"Well, if he keeps making that racket he won't have to miss home any longer, because I'll send him back," Mum says. "Where's your dad? He's supposed to be taking him for a walk before breakfast."

"Ah," Dad says, coming into the kitchen. "Can I have a bit?" He picks up a slice of toast from Mum's plate.

"Hey, that's mine!" she says.

"Sorry, got up late," Dad says, putting on his jacket. "That dog kept me awake whining half the night."

"But you said you were going to take it for a walk—" calls Mum, as he heads for the door.

"Late for work!" Dad says. "Bye."

"Completely irresponsible!" Mum says, but Dad has already gone.

Mum makes me take Sabre for a walk, even though it is totally most likely going to make me late for school. "You wanted a dog. Now you can look after it," she says, for about the five hundredth time this morning.

It isn't till I am trying to put Sabre's lead on that I realise I am not really sure how to take a dog for a walk. I've never done it before. Other people make it look easy, but there's quite a lot to think about. I mean, how far do you take them? And how do you know when they've had enough?

"And don't forget to take a

poo bag," Mum says, stuffing a little plastic bag in my pocket.

"A what?"

"You'll have to pick it up if he goes," she says, shoving me out of the door.

I take Sabre off down the street and after a few minutes I feel quite proud of myself. Everything is going fine and I am walking a dog like a proper owner, and I have even managed to get halfway down our road without one disaster. Then he stops. I give him a bit of a pull on the lead but he won't go any further, and I realise he is doing a poo right there in the middle of the pavement, with people walking past on their way to work and school.

"Sabre. Not here!" I mutter, and give him a firmer tug on his lead, but he doesn't budge until he's finished.

And then he walks away leaving it right in the middle of the pavement for everyone to see! I have to try to pick it up in the  bag. It is a very tricky thing to do, especially when you are holding the lead of a dog who is trying to run off down the road and pulling you off balance. You have to sort of turn the bag inside out and make a grab for it. It could easily become a very unpleasant experience. I manage to sort it out without too much of a disaster and I am feeling quite pleased with myself again for getting quite professional at dog-owning, when I realise that I now have to walk all the way up the road carrying a dog poo in a bag. It is a totally embarrassing thing to have as an accessory. These are the things no one ever tells you about looking after a dog.

After all the dog-walking and poo

stress I am a bit late meeting Zuzanna for school. She is standing outside her house looking at her wrist when I come running up, which is what she does even if she hasn't got a watch on. She is also frowning and it is definitely bordering on a 4.1 on the Zuzanna Frown Scale.

Not good.

"Well?" she says.

"I had to take a dog for a walk. There's more to it than you think."

"Never mind all that. Is your mum going to join the PTA?"

"Oh ... er ... yes, I think so," I mutter.

"Did you ask her?"

"Erm ... you'd really like Sabre! He's very cute. We've got him for a week."

"You didn't ask her, did you?" she says, frowning close to a 4.8. Imminent meltdown.

"No."

"Emily! You are completely irresponsible," Zuzanna says, marching off ahead.

"It runs in the family," I say.

CHAPTER 4

Blue-Sky Thinking

Still Friday

All morning Chloe and Zuzanna are being off-ish with me, and at lunchtime they just sit on the ENDSHIP SEA being moody and moaning about the new clothes they won't get to wear to the disco. I am very glad to hear the bell go for the end of break.

When we get into class, Mrs Lovetofts is moving

the tables around. She has got Amy-Lee Langer and Gross-Out Gavin to help her. This is typical of Mrs Lovetofts. All the nice kids (which is mostly me, I am beginning to think) get stuck outside in the drizzle, while the class bully and the class disgusting person get to stay in the warm and help out. It's so she can keep an eye on them and stop them being bully-ish and disgusting-ish in the playground, but it is totally unfair and not teaching them a lesson at all. If I was a teacher I'd make sure all the annoying children stood out in the drizzle all the time and were only allowed inside once a day, to say sorry for being annoying. That would be a much better idea. I have lots of ideas that would make the world a better place if only I could get someone to listen. Like not opening schools till 10 a.m. to stop people being late because they can't find one shoe which has mysteriously ended up in the washing basket. (That was last week.)

Anyway, Amy-Lee and Gross-Out are not being at all helpful: Amy-Lee is just trying to jam Gross-Out's fingers between the tables, and Gross-Out is trying to burp in Amy-Lee's face.

When Mrs Lovetofts has finally finished getting all the tables as she wants them, they are arranged in a big rectangle in the middle of the room taking up all the space, with three chairs on one side and all the rest of the chairs squashed around the other side, under the window. It is very strange and not good for doing work – or even moving, really.

"Sit down please, class," Mrs Lovetofts says.

Everyone looks around, confused.

"Don't worry, just choose a seat anywhere," she

says. Which is all right for her to say, but it is not very easy to get to anywhere, or even somewhere, at the moment. There is a mass scramble as we all try to get to a chair. It is a bit like musical chairs but with no music or prizes. Or fun.

When everyone has finished climbing over each other or crawling under chairs or apologising to someone they just elbowed in the eye, Mrs Lovetofts says, "Well done, everyone. Now, as you know, this is the last week before half-term and on Wednesday it's the school fete. And, just for fun, we are going to do a very special, new and exciting project ..."

There is a bit of a pause and I am just wondering if she has forgotten what the very special, new and exciting project is when she starts singing: "*Dum dee-dum dee-dum dee-dum dee-dum dee-dum dee-dum duuuum ...*"

I do not think it is a very good time to start singing because everyone is just waiting to find out what the new and exciting project is, and most people probably have their breath completely bated (whatever that means). Mrs Lovetofts must realise this because she stops singing (or maybe it is because Alfie has put his fingers in his ears), and then she says in a strange voice, "Welcome to the boardroom!"

I think it is a voice that is supposed to be deep and scary, but it actually sounds more like she has accidentally swallowed a satsuma, whole. Everyone looks a bit more confused and Daniel Waller's bottom lip starts to wobble.

Mrs Lovetofts continues quickly, in a more normal voice: "Look, the thing is, we're going to have our own version of *The Apprentice*. Just like on TV, with that nice Lord Sweet."

"You mean Lord Sugar, Miss," Joshua says.

"Exactly. You are all my apprentices! We are going to have our own boardroom and I am going to set you a challenge. The team that makes the most money wins. It's going to be such fun!" Mrs Lovetofts claps her hands together and tries to do a little dance, but there's not enough room.

"Miss," Alfie says, "does that mean we are going to be millionaires?"

"No, Alfie. We are going to donate the money raised to a good cause."

"But I'm a good cause. Can't we donate it to me?" Alfie says.

"Now, Alfie, don't be greedy," Mrs Lovetofts says. "We will be donating all the money you make to the winning team's chosen charity. But there will be a little prize for the team leader whose team raises the most money."

There is a general "ooohing" noise as the class gets excited again.

44

"What sort of prize, Miss?" Gracie asks.

Mrs Lovetofts continues: "The winning team leader will get—"

"Chocolate?" Nicole asks.

"No, a—"

"Gift voucher?" Babette asks.

"No, a Jun—

"A junior-sized helicopter and private landing pad?" Alfie asks.

"No. A Juniper Road Primary School Young Business Person of the Year Certificate!" Mrs Lovetofts beams, ignoring the groans. "And everyone on the winning team will also get a Head Teacher's Certificate."

"Ooooh, good," Zuzanna says. "I need one more. I've got seven, and they don't look at all symmetrical lined up on my wall."

And I think, *My display of Head Teacher's Certificates is perfectly symmetrical.* Then again, I only have one.

"But, Miss," Small Emily B. says, "who's going to choose the teams?"

"I've sorted that out already," Mrs Lovetofts says, sounding very pleased with herself for thinking about something in advance for once. "I've got the teams written up on the laptop. Just a minute, and I'll put them up on the whiteboard."

It ends up taking a lot more than a minute as Mrs Lovetofts turns around and realises her laptop is on the other side of the classroom and she can't get out from behind the table.

"Oh, silly me," she says. "I'll have to climb over." There's an alarming moment as she clambers across the tables, knocking over a box of glue sticks and narrowly missing putting her foot through Joshua

Radcliffe's papier-mâché harvest pumpkin. It is not something I have ever seen Lord Sugar do. When she gets to the laptop she finds it isn't plugged in so she has to climb over several more people to get to the power socket, but eventually the teams are up.

I'm with Chloe, Zuzanna, Yeah-Yeah Yasmin and Alfie Balfour. This is not a very good mixture. Chloe will want to be in charge, Zuzanna will want to win, Yasmin will do absolutely nothing except cause an argument and Alfie will just be a complete pain and utterly annoying. I can tell it's going to be a disaster and we haven't even started yet. At least I haven't got Amy-Lee or Gross-Out on my team. In fact, no one has.

"But, Miss, what team am I on?" Gross-Out says.

"Yeah, and me?" Amy-Lee says.

"Ah, well. I'm sure you've all seen Lord Sticky on the telly—"

"Lord Sugar, Miss," Joshua says.

"Yes, him too," Mrs Lovetofts says.  "He always has two helpers, and my helpers are going to be ... Amy-Lee and Gavin!"

Amy-Lee and Gross-Out go to sit in the chairs next to Mrs Lovetofts, looking all smug as if they have just been selected to do something really good, instead of just being kept out of the teams because Mrs Lovetofts knows they'll mess everything up.

"Now then, class, settle down," Mrs Lovetofts says, once she has stopped Amy-Lee and Gross-Out arguing about which one is Karren Brady. "You need to get into your teams, decide on a team leader and a team name. Then I will give you your team challenge and you will need to put your plan into action."

There is a bit of a confused silence and then everyone starts talking at once and trying to find their team members.

"Just a minute!" Mrs Lovetofts says. "We need to put the tables back first."

Unfortunately, putting the tables back takes till nearly home time and results in two people (Gracie McKenzie and Amy-Lee Langer) having to go to the secretary for cold compresses on their foreheads, and one person (Gross-Out Gavin) having to go to see Mr Meakin for carrying a chair "without due care and attention". When we finally get to sit in our groups, there are only five minutes left.

"Just sort your teams out and I will give you the challenge on Monday," Mrs Lovetofts says.

"OK," Chloe says. "First we have to choose a team leader. I would like to put myself forward, as the obvious choice."

"Obvious?" Zuzanna says.

"*Oui*. On the basis that I have considerable business experience."

"Do you?" I say.

"Of course. When I was at my old school, Mag Hall, we did Business Studies every day."

"And I suppose Richard Branson came in to advise you?" Zuzanna says.

"Oh – have I told you this before?" Chloe says. "Also, of course, I have a lot of experience gained from my mum's international business-type job."

"Chloe, your mum is a cleaner," Zuzanna says.

"Anyway, I will clearly be the best person for the job," Chloe says.

"Why?" Alfie says.

Chloe snatches up a piece of paper that Mrs Lovetofts has just put on the table. "Because I have the worksheet so I am the only one who knows what to do. Does anyone else want to put themselves forward? *Non?*"

"I suppose if you really want to do it," Zuzanna says. "But you'd better do a good job. I totally need that Head Teacher's Certificate."

"Good," Chloe says. "Anyone else?"

"No." I sigh.

"Not likely," Alfie says.

"Yeah," Yasmin says.

"Really?" Zuzanna says. "You want to be team leader, Yasmin?"

"No, I was just sayin' yeah," Yasmin says.

"So, you don't want to be team leader?"

"Yeah."

We are all still trying to work out what Yasmin means when Chloe takes advantage of the confusion and announces, "Right then, it's me. My first appointment is going to be Zuzanna as Chief Writer-down of Everything, because she has the best writing and a posh pen."

"What about the rest of us?" Alfie says. "What are we going to be?"

"Yeah," Yasmin says.

"Emily can be Chief Finder-out of Things because she likes reading books and weird stuff like that, and Yasmin and Alfie can be Chief ... umm ...

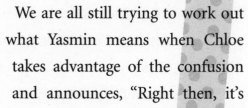

other people. Right, now let's get on." Chloe looks at the worksheet. "First of all, we need to decide on a name for our team. Let's have some blue-sky thinking on this."

"Some what?" I say.

"It's a saying, Emily, among business people. Just try to hang on to my coat-tails, here."

"What coat-tails?"

Zuzanna gives me a shrug which I think means she doesn't know what's going on either, but she still writes it down.

"Right, team, we need a name that shows our character and determination to succeed in a tough business environment," Chloe says.

"I'm not sure Year Six, Juniper Road Primary, really counts as a tough business environment," I say.

Chloe slaps the table with her hand, making everyone jump. "Don't be negative, Emily. The number one rule of business is 'Be positive.'"

"I'm not being negative," I say. "I just said—"

"Let's not get side-tracked, Emily. The number one rule in business is, 'Don't get side-tracked.'"

"But you just said it was, 'Be positive,'" Alfie says.

"Exactly," Chloe says. "'Positively don't get side-tracked.' Now then, any suggestions for the team name?"

"How about Team Win?" Zuzanna says.

"No," Chloe says. "Next."

"Team Dynamic?" I suggest.

"No," Chloe says. "Next."

"Team Totally Terrific?" Alfie says.

"No," Chloe says.

"Look, you can't just keep saying 'no'. We should have a vote or something," Alfie says. "We're supposed to be a team."

"Yeah," Yasmin says.

"Brilliant! I love it!" Chloe says.

"Well done, Yasmin. Team Yeah! It shows a can-do attitude and sounds really positive," she says, giving me a hard stare. "We are Team Yeah!"

"We can't call ourselves Team Yeah," I say. "That just sounds silly."

"Yes," Zuzanna says. "It doesn't mean anything. It might as well be in French."

"Fantastic idea, Zuzanna! We are not Team Yeah, we are Team *Oui*!"

"Team *Oui*?" I say.

"Yes," Chloe says. "It shows our international dimension. Business is all about being international. Just ask my mum."

"Chloe, your mum is a cleaner," Zuzanna says.

"That name's even more stupid," I say. "We can't call ourselves that!"

But Chloe can't hear because she is standing up and punching the air shouting, "Go *Oui*! Go

Oui!" at all the other teams, who are looking a bit scared.

"We're supposed to vote," I say, but my voice is drowned out by the home-time bell.

"OK, Team *Oui!* Keep thinking those blue-sky thoughts. And on Monday I want you all to have a deliverable to bring to the table," Chloe says, slapping down her hand and making everyone jump again.

"A what?" Zuzanna says. "Can you spell that?" but Chloe has already left.

Zuzanna and I walk home together.

"You should come round and see Sabre," I say. "He's really cute."

"I might another time," Zuzanna says, "but I

can't tonight. My mum's going to the emergency
PTA meeting and I'm going with her ... to show
my support." She looks at me sternly.

"I'll ask Mum when I get home," I say.

CHAPTER 5

The Crow and the Lizard

Friday evening

When I get close to my house I can see the lights are on in Mrs Theodopolis's-house-which-isn't-Mrs-Theodopolis's-house-any-more. I am trying to see what is going on without actually turning my head and looking, in case someone sees me and thinks I'm interested which, of course, I am but I'm not letting anyone know. It is very difficult to look without turning your head and it makes your eyes ache and it also makes you not pay attention to where you are going and fall over a box that is on the pavement, which is not where a box should be.

It isn't a very big fall – it's one of those falls that is more embarrassing than painful, especially as a woman rushes out of the house shouting, "Oh, dear, oh, how awful, are you all right? Griff, Griff, come out here! This poor child has hurt herself on your box." And she leans over me, all big orange skirt and gold bangles and long hair.

"*My* box?" says a very tall, thin man, coming down the path. "But, as you know my sweetness, what is mine is yours." He is wearing a purple velvet suit and has longish grey hair and a beard. He does a little bow to me and says, "Griff Izzard, at your service."

"Really, Griff, it's time you got rid of this old thing anyway," says the woman, and she picks up the thing that has fallen out of the box and stands it on the pavement.

This is when I realise our new neighbours are not normal.

Sitting on the pavement is a big, black, stuffed bird with a hooked beak and black claws. It stares right at me with glass eyes and too many feathers.

By this time I am trying to edge along the pavement to my house on my bottom, whilst biting hard on my lip to stop myself yelling, "Mum! Help! Nutters!"

Suddenly there is a screech of tyres and a car pulls up. Someone bowls out of the door to rescue me. Unfortunately, it is Gran.

"Emily! What are you doing on the ground?"

"I ... er ... umm."

"Neighbourhood Watch. What is going on here?" Gran says, turning to Griff and the woman.

"I think she fell," says the woman, fluttering her hands and making her bangles jangle. "Over that." She points to the box.

"A likely story," says Gran. "Back away from my grandchild now!"

"It's an old, stuffed crow," says Griff.

"I beg your pardon? How dare you!" says Gran, and swings her handbag in his general direction.

"Mother! Stop assaulting Mr Izzard!" Mum is standing at the gate with her hands on her hips.

"Who?" Gran says, stopping mid swing.

"Mr and Mrs Izzard." Mum sighs. "Our new neighbours."

"Oh, really?" says Gran, dropping her arm and holding out her hand. "Maureen Scrutton. Retired school lunch supervisor and Neighbourhood Watch coordinator. Pleased to meet you."

Mr Izzard takes Gran's hand carefully, like it's

some sort of trap. "Griff Izzard. And this is my wife, Wanda."

"Shall we all have a cup of tea?" Mum says. "Clover's awake now, if you'd like to see her, Wanda—?"

"Do you have lemongrass and ginger?" Wanda says.

"Oh. No. Probably just PG Tips," Mum says, looking a bit embarrassed. Then she snaps, "Emily, get up off the ground. You're making your school trousers dirty."

That is so typical of my mum – like trousers are important when I have just been in a near-tragedy with a cardboard box and a dead bird. But at least no one is bothering me now: they are all going up our front path chattering away as if they've been friends for years.

I get up and brush the dust from my trousers

and I am just about to follow them in when I notice a head. It is looking at me from over the top of the hedge. It is very pale and it has big, round, staring eyes surrounded by lots of black eyeliner.

It moves slowly around the hedge towards me and I am completely hoping it will have the rest of a person attached. Luckily, it does, and I am very relieved, even if that person is a strange-looking girl with straight black hair and black lipstick.

"Hi," I say. "Do you live here too?"

"You must be Emily," she says.

"Correct," I say, with a smile.

But she doesn't smile back. Just keeps staring.

"What's your name?" I ask.

"Lena," she says. "Izzard," and sort of drops her head to one side as if she expects me to say something.

"Right," I say, because I suddenly can't think of anything to say which doesn't include the word "lizard" and, given the look on her face, that probably wouldn't be a good idea. There is a bit of an awkward silence while she stares at me and then I say, "Yes, well. Do you want to come in and find your mum and dad?"

"Not really. Goodbye, Emily," she says in a way which makes me think she might be about to kill me with a zombie death grip or something. She takes a step towards me and I sort of jump back a bit, but she just bends down and picks up the stuffed crow. "Come on, Barney. You don't want to hang around on the pavement where anyone can kick you." She looks right at me.

"Well, bye then," I say, walking away quickly.

I know Mrs Theodopolis smelled of broccoli and shouted at the postman if he forgot to shut the gate, but I'm beginning to wish she had never left.

By the time I get in, Gran is chatting to Griff about something or other, while Wanda is already bangling and jangling over Clover's baby seat. Her long, dark hair (Wanda's, not Clover – she is *still* totally bald, something I would worry about if I had time) keeps poking Clover in the eye.

"Oh, she's lovely!" she says. "They grow up so fast, don't they? I'm sure it was only yesterday when little Lena was this size." Which makes me think, *She must have had a lot of dinner since yesterday.* She leans right over Clover again and says, "Coo-

coo, little baby … coo-coo," which is something I don't think Clover will like.

"Coo-coo— aaaaargh!"

Thought not.

Clover has got hold of Wanda's hair and given it a good pull, which is her way of saying, "Stop with the poking in the eye and the coo-coo stuff!"

Wanda makes a lot of fuss trying to get Clover to let go: "Nice baby. Nice baby. Let go now."

"Yee-haa," Clover says and hangs on tight, until Mum comes to the rescue.

"I don't think I'll have that tea after all," Wanda says, rubbing her head. "I'd better get back. Lena's on her own." And I think, *She doesn't have to worry. One glare from Lena's black-ringed eyes would be enough to make any burglar run home to his mummy.*

Mum walks Wanda to the door nattering about

yoga, but Weird Griff is still stuck in conversation with Gran. In fact, she is chatting away to him as if they've been best friends for life. You would never guess that five minutes ago she was trying to do him damage with her handbag.

Sabre seems to have taken quite a liking to Weird Griff too, and is curled up on his lap.

"He likes you," Gran says.

"Oh, yes." Griff smiles. "I'm fond of animals."

"So, what do you do?" Gran says.

"Oh, I dabble," Griff says, looking longingly towards the front door. I don't understand what he means by "dabble". Dabble in what? Muddy ponds? But it doesn't bother Gran: she is only trying to get being polite out of the way so she can talk about herself.

"That's very interesting," she says. "Now, I was born in—"

Griff looks around for someone to get him out

of there, but it's his own fault for getting involved in the first place.

"Oh, is that the time? Perhaps I should help Wanda with the unpacking," he says, attempting to stand up with Sabre still on his lap.

Gran slaps her hand on his shoulder. "Don't be silly, Griff. Five minutes won't hurt. Now, where were we?" Griff casts me a desperate look as Gran says, "Never mind, I'll start again."

And I think, *This is a very good time to take Sabre for a walk.*

I have noticed that when you have a dog, everyone else with a dog talks to you. It is very strange. There are old ladies with young dogs and young men with old dogs, and all sorts of other combinations.

Some people even have two or three dogs. But whatever sort of person they are and whatever sort of dog they've got, they all say "Hello." I have walked up and down our street loads of times without a dog and not been spoken to by anyone; now, suddenly, I am ultra-popular. The trouble is it means that everyone is watching you, too, so when Sabre does a poo there is no chance of just kicking it under a hedge, and I have to do the whole lead-and-poo-bag-juggling thing again. To be honest, I am getting a bit fed up with this dog-walking stuff, and I've only done it twice.

CHAPTER 6

Disco Disaster!

Even more Friday

When I get back it is all quiet, and everyone seems to have gone. I go into the kitchen to find Mum with a packet of sausages in one hand and a tin of tuna in the other.

"How does sausage and tuna bake sound?" she asks.

"Disgusting," I say.

"Yeah, that's what I thought."

"Mum, have you seen my school newsletter?"

"No, why? Have you lost it?"

"No, I mean, would you like to read it?"

"Not right now," Mum says, which means not ever.

"Well, tell you what, I'll read it to you," I say.

"Good idea," she says, throwing the sausages into a frying pan.

I go to find my schoolbag just as Dad gets in.

"Hello," he says. "Something smells nice." Which is his way of trying to get Mum into a good mood.

"It's just sausages," Mum says. "I haven't had time to do anything else. I've had to look after a baby and a dog all day. And it weed on the rug. Again."

"Which is why I bought you these," Dad says,

pulling a bunch of flowers from behind his back.

Mum's face softens. "That's very nice," she says, "but the point is you were supposed to take him for a walk—"

"I know," Dad says, grinning. "I'm completely irresponsible."

"Just keep an eye on those sausages while I try to find a tin of beans," Mum says.

I go to get the newsletter from my bag in the hall and bring it back to the kitchen to read. I skip most of it until I get to the important bit. "Listen, Mum, '... it may not be possible to run the school half-term disco this year. An emergency meeting of the Parent Teachers' Association will be held this Friday evening to discuss possible fund-raising activities. New members warmly welcomed.'"

"Oh no, the sausages are burning!" Mum says. "Keith! You're supposed to be keeping an eye on these!" she yells to Dad, who has wandered into the other room.

"Am I?" Dad says, coming back into the kitchen. Mum glares at him and I think I had better get this PTA thing sorted out before she gets *really* stressed out.

"The thing is, if more parents don't join the PTA then we won't be able to have the school disco and that will be really sad, won't it?" I say.

"Tragic," Mum says from inside the cupboard, where she is making another attempt to find a tin of beans.

"Not as tragic as this dinner," Dad mutters.

"What?" Mum says.

"Nothing," Dad says, winking at me.

"But can't you join, Mum?" I ask.

"We'll have to have peas," Mum says.

"Mum?"

"What?"

"Can't you join the PTA?"

"The PTA?" Mum snaps. "As if I haven't got enough to do! I've got the baby, the house, the dog, the Allotment Club, Gran ..."

"Gran doesn't take any looking after," I say.

"No, but I have to schedule in a lot of time for chatting to her."

"Mum's very busy, Em," Dad says. "She hasn't even got time to burn the dinner properly."

Mum makes a sort of strangly sound and throws the tea towel at him.

It's lucky she didn't find a can of beans or he might have had that too.

"I'll tell you what," Dad says. "Why don't *I* join the PTA?"

"You?" Mum and I say together.

"Yes, why not?" Dad says. "I am a parent too, you know. Equality and all that. Pass me the letter." I hand Dad the newsletter. "There's a meeting tonight – I'll go to that," he says. "You see,

I'm not completely irresponsible. Never fear, Emily, the disco will go on!"

After dinner, Dad changes into a clean shirt and heads off to school. I am in total shock. The only time my dad ever goes to my school is for parents' evening, and even then he doesn't listen. I have a feeling I should worry ... but then again, what could go wrong?

I go up to my room to see Wavey Cat. Wavey Cat was a present from my first-best friend, Bella, before she went to live in Wales. He is very useful for good luck-type things. Although he doesn't always do it quite like you expect.

I flick his paw and say, "Wavey Cat. Please can we have a school disco?"

I know it's not a massive wish and I probably should be wishing for something important like world peace and helping out the United Nations. But then again, he's not a very big cat and the United Nations don't have to put up with Zuzanna.

A bit later, Mum takes Clover up to bed. I am just having a nice bit of peace and quiet watching TV when Dad gets back. He comes bounding into the living room looking very pleased with himself, which is always a bad sign.

"Guess what, Emily?" he says. "Great news. The disco is back on!"

"Really? That's brilliant!"

"Yes, and I was the one who sorted it all out."

"Were you?"

"Yes. To get DJ Derek Diamond for the disco they need at least £100."

"And you came up with a really good fund-raising idea?" I say, feeling rather proud of my dad for once. *Wait till Zuzanna hears that he saved the disco.*

"Better than that, Emily. I had a really good money-*saving* idea." He grins broadly. "I've agreed to be the DJ instead!"

"You've *what*?" I say, because I am trying to give my brain time to work out another meaning to what Dad has just said. One that doesn't involve me having to voluntarily put myself into care.

"Yep. Just call me DJ Dad! One school disco saved!"

"But ... how? Why? I mean ... you *can't!*"

"Of course I can. I've got records and a record player – or, should I say, 'a deck'?"

"A deck?"

"Yes, it's DJ speak – I'm getting quite into it already. I'm going to spin some discs and lay down some happening beats," he says, trying to do a robot dance across the living room floor.

I feel faint. "Dad, no one wants to hear your old records!"

"Of course they will. The Megatronics always get the crowd going."

"Yes. Going home!"

"Griff likes them, too."

"Who?"

"Griff Izzard, our new neighbour. I just met him on the way back. Nice chap. He said how much he enjoyed the music I was playing the other evening. Apparently he's a big fan of The Megatronics.

In fact, he's just agreed to be my assistant DJ. Apparently he's got some great discs himself."

"Assistant DJ? But, but—" Really, there are too many disasters happening at once for me to keep up.

"He's going to join the PTA."

"But he can't." I see a faint ray of hope. "He's not a parent."

"Yes, he is. Lena is joining Year Five on Monday."

And with that my last sliver of hope completely packs its bags and leaves.

"Yes," Mum says, coming back downstairs, "I said we could all walk in together. Wanda isn't sure of the way and Lena's a bit shy, apparently."

"Shy! She's not shy. She's just ... weird."

"Apparently she got bullied at her last school."

"Well, that's hardly surprising," I say. "She wears black nail varnish and carries a dead crow around."

"Emily, that's not a very kind attitude," Mum replies, and she heads for the kitchen, closely followed by Dad who is singing: "Let's all have a disc-oh, Let's all have a disc-oh," and practising his dance moves.

Emily says: Bella. Are you there??

Bella says: Hi. How's things?

Emily says: Awful. We have new neighbours. They are total-tastically weird. The girl is called Lena. I think she might be an actual alien, or a zombie, or vampire - or all three. And their pet is a dead crow.

Bella says: At least that's interesting. Our neighbours are sheep.

Emily says: Even worse – Dad's going to be the DJ at the school disco.

Bella says: Noooooooooooooooo.

Emily says: Yeeeeeeeeeeeeeeeeeeeeees.

Bella says: Nooooooooooooooooooooooooooo.

Emily says: Yeeeeeeees ... I need your help. What am I going to do?

Bella says: Ummmmm ... You could lend him some CDs?

Emily says: I've only got *The Lion King* and *Super Songs for Six Year Olds*.

Bella says: iPod?

Emily says: I dropped it down the toilet, remember? Anyway, he wants to play his records.

Bella says: But why is he being the DJ?

Emily says: Because they haven't got enough money for a proper one.

Bella says: You'd better hope they find some money from somewhere.

Emily says: I am hoping. I'm hoping really hard but I don't think that will be enough.

Bella says: You never know your luck - perhaps he'll break his leg playing football and end up in hospital.

Emily says: Good thinking. I'll keep my fingers crossed. And on Monday I've got to walk to school with Loopy Lena.

Bella says: Maybe she'll kill you with a zombie death stare and then you won't have to worry any more.

As far as cheering-up lines go, that's not the best Bella's ever come up with.

I go up to my room to see Wavey Cat. "Wavey Cat, you've got it a bit wrong. When I said I wanted a disco, I didn't mean get my dad to do it." I flick his paw. "Wavey Cat, are you listening? We need a disco with really good music. We need a proper DJ. I need a miracle."

It wasn't a great weekend. First of all Sabre ate my advent calendar (I start them very early). At least he only got the current one, but I've lost two weeks of chocolate. Then Mum told me off when he was sick.

On Saturday night, Mum went next door to do yoga with Wanda. She suggested that I might like to come and see Lena but I think she got the message when I said I'd rather eat slugs. Weird Griff came round to see Dad. They played loads of old crackly records all evening saying things like, "Amazing track!" and "Listen to that bass," and "What a fantastic drum solo." I decided to go to bed early and put a pillow over my head. But then I got such a warm head I needed a glass of water so I came back downstairs. Dad and Griff didn't even notice me, they were so into their music. They were playing The Megatronics. Again.

"It will be brilliant if we finally get to see them," Dad said. "They must be all in their fifties by now."

"At least," said Griff. "But they still play some amazing music."

"Too right," Dad said. "'Laser Love' is my all-time favourite track. It's going to be really strange hearing the lads playing it on Friday night."

What does he mean, "hearing the lads playing it on Friday night"? Friday night is the school disco.

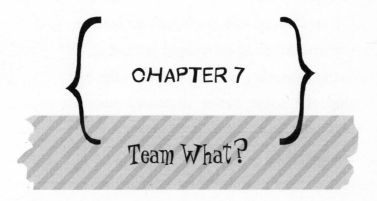

CHAPTER 7

Team What?

Monday morning

It is not even properly daytime yet and we are running late. We are supposed to leave at 8.23 a.m. but Mum is still not sorted and it is 8.26 a.m. already. (See how much better it would be if school started at 10 a.m.?) Zuzanna will be in a huff and that's before she even gets started on the disco disaster – her mum is bound to have told her. I'm surprised I haven't had one of her stroppy texts already.

I don't know why Mum can't get ready on time. After eleven years of practising being a mother, you'd have thought she'd be a bit better organised by now. She only had to get Clover ready, make my packed lunch (which is basically an apple, a bag of crisps and a peanut butter sandwich chucked in a bag – not gourmet cuisine or anything) and clean the puddle off the kitchen floor where Sabre had another accident.

Apparently he whined all night again. It's sad really, because he is probably missing Daisy, but Mum doesn't have any patience with animal emotions. She just keeps moaning about not getting any sleep. I didn't hear him whining at all.

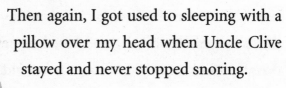

Then again, I got used to sleeping with a pillow over my head when Uncle Clive stayed and never stopped snoring.

"We'll take Sabre with us," Mum says. "I daren't leave him behind, he'll probably wee on the rug again." She hands me the lead and bounces Clover's buggy out of the front door.

Lena is waiting for us by the gate with her mum. Really, she should be leaning against the gate because that would go with her name, but she is not. She is standing very straight and staring at me in a very staring-ly sort of way. I can't believe  she is wearing black eyeliner and nail varnish to school. She's bound to get told off. At least she doesn't have her black lipstick on, but she does have a black headband, black tights and big black clumpy shoes. She looks like she's going to a vampire party.

"It's so kind of you to walk in with us," Wanda says. "It'll be nice for Lena to arrive with someone she knows. She's a bit shy, aren't you, honey?"

And I think, *It might be nice for her but it won't*

be nice for me. I don't want to get stuck with a freak-tastic Year Five to look after.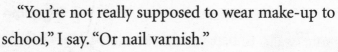

Lena gives me a thin smile, which makes me do a little shudder. I try to hang behind a bit but soon Mum and Wanda are nattering away about yoga again, and Lena is walking next to me.

"You're not really supposed to wear make-up to school," I say. "Or nail varnish."

"I didn't realise you were the head teacher," she says.

"I'm just telling you so you don't get into trouble," I say. *And also because it's very embarrassing walking to school with someone who looks like they stepped out of a scary movie*, I think.

 Lena clumps along beside me not saying anything, which is just about as uncomfortable as when she does.

I am very relieved when I see Zuzanna waiting outside her house. "I'll see you later. I'm going to walk with my friend now," I say.

"She doesn't look very pleased to see you," Lena says, which is true.

Zuzanna is doing a 3.6 frown. Not too bad – it's probably because no one has informed her that we have extra company on our walk to school this morning.

I tug on Sabre's lead sharply and walk towards Zuzanna with a cheery wave. Even walking with Zuzanna in a bad mood is better than spending any more time with Lena.

"Who's that?" asks Zuzanna, pointing towards Lena, who has gone to walk with her mum.

"My new neighbour," I say. "Dracu-Lena."

"Weird shoes," Zuzanna says.

"Weird girl," I say. "Come on, let's walk ahead."

"Did you hear about the disco?" Zuzanna says.

"Nice day, isn't it?" I say.

"Emily, I asked if you heard about the disco?"

"Er . . ." I sigh. "Yes. Look, I'm really sorr—"

"Great news, isn't it?" Zuzanna says.

"What? Is it?"

"Yes, haven't you heard? Mum says they've found a DJ and they're going ahead with it after all. I can wear my new dress! Did I tell you I've got a new dress?"

"Did your mum say any more about this new DJ?" I ask.

"No. To be honest, she couldn't go to the meeting, she had a headache, but she got a text to say it's all sorted out. Apparently they've got a DJ to do it for free. I expect it's DJ Derek Diamond, as usual. He probably loves doing the discos so much he doesn't want any money – they *are* really fun, aren't they?"

"Usually," I say.

"I can't wait. I've got a new dress. Did I tell you? Oooh, look, we're in Cedar Road!"

"Er, yes. We come this way every day."

"There it is, look. Number forty-seven." Zuzanna points to a slightly scruffy-looking house across the street and clasps her hands to her chest. "Isn't it fantastic?"

"Is it?"

"I only found out last night. Kit from the NV Boyz – his granny used to live there. He's actually slept in that house."

"I bet he wouldn't sleep in it now," I say.

At school, Chloe and Zuzanna can't stop talking about the disco.

"I am totally putting in a request for them to play everything by the NV Boyz," Zuzanna says. And I think, *That should be easy, because they've only done two songs: "The Only Girl" and "Superstar".*

Then I remember my dad hasn't even got those and I wonder how easy it would be to stow away on a ship to the Arctic.

"I still can't decide what look I'm going to go for," Chloe says. "Where did you say you got your dress from, Zuzanna?"

"I'm not sure. My mum got it."

"Probably Tesco then. Never mind."

"What are you wearing on Friday, Emily?"

"Probably some furry boots and a fleecy anorak," I say, thinking, *I will need*

*to stay warm when I have
to live in an igloo.*

"Emily, what are you *totalement* on about?"

"Oh. Er … I mean, I don't know yet," I say.

"I don't know either," Chloe says. "I have nothing to wear."

"You got a new dress last week, Chloe," I say.

"Exactly. It is *so* last week. I am totally over geek-chic."

"Well, there's not long left to find something," Zuzanna says. "It's too exciting."

I wish they would stop talking about it – it's making me feel ill. I am even glad when Mrs Lovetofts starts humming, "*Dum dee-dum dee-dum dee-dum dee-dum …*" and claps her hands for silence. "Now then, team leaders," she says. "I need to know what you decided on for your team names. Small Emily B. – what's your team name?"

"Succeed," Small Emily B. says.

"Very good," beams Mrs Lovetofts, writing it on the board. "Team Succeed – and I'm sure you will! And Joshua, your team is—?"

"Achieve, Miss," Joshua says.

"Excellent," Mrs Lovetofts says. "I'm sure you will achieve great things. And finally, Chloe?"

"*Oui*." Chloe says.

Mrs Lovetofts frowns. "Your team name, please, Chloe."

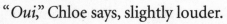

"*Oui*," Chloe says, slightly louder.

Mrs Lovetofts frowns even more, which must be quite difficult for her because she only really knows how to smile. "Did you understand the question, Chloe?"

"*Oui*," Chloe says. "As in 'Yeah'."

"Yeah," Yasmin says.

"And it's a 'yeah' from me, too," Alfie says, and does a snorty laugh.

I think I'd better intervene in case our whole team gets fired before we've even started. "We are called Team *Oui*, Miss," I say. "O-U-I. It's meant to be positive and, er ... international-ish."

"Oh, I see." Mrs Lovetofts laughs. "Team *Oui*. Well, it's certainly original and I'm sure you will ... hmm. Anyway, let's move on. Can you let me know which good causes you would like the proceeds to go to, if your team wins?"

With all the fussing about the name, our group has completely forgotten to think about this.

"Emily," Chloe hisses. "You didn't sort out the good cause."

"You're team leader," I hiss back.

"I can't do everything on my own. You're Chief Finder-out of Things. You should have found something out and then told Zuzanna, who should have written it down and then brought it to me for an executive decision. That's why I employ you."

"You don't employ—" I start to say, but Mrs Lovetofts says, "Quieten down, please, class. Right. Team Succeed. Who would you like to nominate as a good cause?"

"We would like the money to go to the Silver Years Retirement Home," Small Emily B. says. "My nana lives there. She really likes it. Except for this woman who smells of broccoli and shouts at the postman."

"Very good idea," Mrs Lovetofts says. "Team Achieve?"

"We would like to donate to the school football team, so they can get new shirts," says Joshua. "The ones we have now are ancient."

"Excellent idea," Mrs Lovetofts says. "Team *Oui*, would you like to nominate a good cause?"

And suddenly my sliver of hope comes back in the front door and starts unpacking again.

"We haven't really thought—" Chloe starts.

"The PTA!" I say.

"What?" Chloe says.

"Can we donate to the PTA so they can have enough money to, say, put on events, or discos or something, Miss?"

"Very good. The PTA is always trying to raise funds," Mrs Lovetofts says, writing it down on the whiteboard.

"Emily," Chloe says, "you do know I'm the team leader? You can't go off like a loose cannon in a china shop making up your own rules about good causes."

"Sorry, Chloe," I say, "but sometimes I have to do some blue-sky thinking of my own."

"Excellent ideas so far, teams," Mrs Lovetofts says. "I'm sure you will raise lots of money, and one of these causes will be very grateful."

And I say, "Definitely!" much louder than I mean to, and everyone laughs, but I don't really mind because now at least I have a plan.

"Now for your challenge," Mrs Lovetofts says, and switches to her swallowed-satsuma voice again.

 "You are to make something suitable for selling to the mums and dads at the school fete on Wednesday. You each have a twenty-pound budget you can spend for materials. But, don't forget, whatever costs you have will come off your final total profit. In other words, don't spend too much! Ready, teams? Off you go!"

There is not much going off. I

think most of us are a bit baffled. With all the build-up, I thought we would be at least designing a space rocket. In fact, I was thinking a space rocket would be quite useful if I couldn't find an Arctic icebreaker by Friday.

"But what sort of thing, Miss?" Babette says.

"That's up to you – let's see your entrepreneurial sides in action!"

"Can you spell that, Miss?" Zuzanna says.

Chloe stands up at the head of our table with a ruler in her hand. "Right, Team *Oui!*" she says, pointing the ruler at each of us in turn. "I am so going to be Juniper Road Primary School Young Business Person of the Year, and you are going to help me. So, let's get all hands on deck for this activity and make sure we are rowing in the same direction."

"You can't row if your hands are on deck," Alfie

says, but Chloe gives him a hard stare and he looks down and starts picking bits of breakfast cereal off his jumper.

"So, ideas, please. What shall we make?"

"Bookmarks?" I say, then I realise we are never going to make any money selling bookmarks. "No. Forget that," I say.

"I already have," Chloe says, rolling her eyes.

"How about baking something?" Zuzanna says. "Like cakes, or biscuits?"

"Are you mad?" Chloe says, slapping the table with her ruler and making everyone jump. "Do you remember the last time we tried to cook? Emily totally ruined it with her mouldy eggs. The last thing we need is Emily poisoning the whole school."

"That was not my fault!" I say.

Zuzanna nods. "Hmm. Actually, I think she's got a point, Emily. No baking."

"What about chocolates?" I say. "We could make

some nice boxes and put chocolates in them. Everyone likes chocolate."

"My dad doesn't," says Alfie. "He likes parsnips, though."

I am getting a headache. "We can't sell parsnips, can we? No one comes to a school fete to buy a parsnip."

"I would," Alfie says. "To give to my dad."

"What we need is something that everyone buys, that's easy to do and that we can charge a lot more for than it costs to make," I say.

"*Excusez moi*, Emily," Chloe says. "I think you are forgetting who is team leader again. What we need," she says, "is something that everyone buys, that's easy to do and that we can charge a lot more for than it costs to make."

"Calendars?" Zuzanna says.

"Boooooring," Chloe says. "Like, no one cares what day it is unless it's your birthday."

"Birthday! Yes! How about cards?" Zuzanna says. "Everyone buys birthday cards, they're cheap to make and we can charge at least 50p each if they're nice."

Chloe looks a little bit annoyed. "Yes, well, that's actually a very good idea," she says. "I was waiting to see if anyone would think of that."

"We need to come up with a design," I say.

"Flowers?" Zuzanna says.

"My mum hates flowers," Yasmin says. "She says they smell."

"It's got to be something that appeals to dads as well," I say. "Usually cards for men have footballs or cars or something on."

"How about parsnips?" Alfie says.

"Perhaps," Zuzanna says, "we should all make a list of the things our mums and dads like. That way we can see if we agree on anything."

"Good idea," Chloe says. "All this talk of vegetables is making me feel ill again."

My dad's favourite stuff
  Football
  Copper pipes
  Tea
  The Megatronics
  Playing the mop

This is basically all I can think of that my dad likes. I was going to put down "Bananas", but I thought that might upset Chloe again. I know it's not a vegetable, but I don't think she likes fruit much, either.

My mum's favourite things
    gardening
    Seeds (I'm hoping Chloe won't get
  stressed about seeds growing into
vegetables.)
  Tea
  Chocolate biscuits
  going to bed

It has taken me ages to think of those things. My mum doesn't really like anything, much. I don't think she has time. This *Apprentice* stuff is harder than it looks.

After about ten minutes Chloe shouts, "Back to the table, team!" which is a bit pointless as we are all sitting around the table already. "Now then, can I see the lists, please?"

Everyone puts their lists in the middle of the table and Chloe reads them out. Chloe's own list says:

What my (step) dad likes
    Very expensive watches
    Very expensive cars
    Very expensive shirts
    Tea (Very expensive is good, but
PG Tips will do.)

What my mum likes
    Same as my dad, plus travelling

internationally for her high-powered job.

"The only thing high-powered about your mum's job is her vacuum cleaner," Zuzanna says.

Chloe ignores her and carries on with the lists. Zuzanna's list says:

My dad likes:
  Chocolate
  Golf
  Radio 4
  Tea

My mum likes:
  Abba
  Cooking
  Tea
  Working very hard for the PTA

Alfie's list says:

My dad's favourite things
   Parsnips
   Birds
   Tea

My mum's favourite things
   Antiques Roadshow
   Ironing
   Tomato soup
   Drinking tea

Yasmin's list says:

Can't be bothered – this is rubbish.

"OK," Chloe says. "I have collated the results of this market research exercise and I think they are pretty conclusive."

"Really?" I say.

"Definitely," Chloe says. "We will make a range of birthday cards featuring ... teapots."

"Teapots!"

"But who's going to buy them?" Zuzanna says.

"People who like tea, of course!" Chloe says. "Which, according to the market research we have just completed, is everyone, basically. Probably even your parents, Yasmin." She fixes Yasmin with one of her steely glares.

"Yeah," Yasmin says.

"But you can't have cards with teapots on!" Zuzanna says.

"Zuzanna," Chloe says sternly, "do you want to be team leader?"

"Yes, OK then," Zuzanna says.

"Well, you can't, because I already am," Chloe says.

"Yeah," Yasmin says.

"Thank you, Yasmin," Chloe says. "It's nice to have a supportive colleague," and she smiles at her. Yasmin looks a bit confused.

"But what are we going to make them out of?" Alfie says.

"Well, I would have thought someone else could work that out. I *do* seem to be having to think of everything myself," Chloe says.

"I suppose we'll have to buy some card," I say. "It could turn out to be quite expensive."

"No expenses!" Chloe says. "You heard what Mrs Lovetofts said. It will come off our final total."

"But we can't make cards without card!" Zuzanna says.

"Leave it to me," Chloe says. "I'm sure I can get – I mean, *source*, some somewhere."

"Two minutes," Mrs Lovetofts says.

"No worries," Chloe says. "We've finished over here. In fact, we have time for a team hug."

"A what?" I say.

"A team hug, to help us bond together. Number one rule of business, Emily, is to get your team to bond." And before I can stop her she has dragged me into a big, huggy circle with Alfie on one side and Yasmin in the other. I feel like the filling in a weirdo sandwich and I am really hoping Alfie hasn't still got nits.

At lunch I go to sit on the ENDSHIP SEA. Zuzanna is having her clarinet lesson and Chloe has gone off saying she's got "something to sort out", so I am on my own. I don't mind, though. Sometimes it's nice to have some peace and quiet, especially after a morning being bossed around by Chloe.

I am just trying to get excited about a peanut butter sandwich when I hear a sound from behind me. I turn around to see Loopy Lena standing very close, holding a book in her hand.

"Hi," I say, trying to make it sound like, "Go away, please."

Lena doesn't answer, and she doesn't go away.

"Did you want something?" I say.

"I'm just standing here, reading. It's a free country, isn't it?"

"Why aren't you over there with the girls in your year?" I ask.

"I'm all right on my own."

"Oh. Right," I say, and I think, *Well, why don't you go away, then?*

I go back to eating my lunch and she just sort of lurks about, doing her starey thing, so I am very relieved when Chloe calls across the playground

114

and comes over, and Lena the Lizard runs off.

"Was that girl wearing black nail varnish?" Chloe asks.

"Yes. She's my new neighbour. She's totally strange."

"Why did she run away? Is she really shy?"

"I don't know, but I wish she'd run away from me more often."

I am actually glad that we get back to normal lessons for the afternoon. It should be fun doing *The Apprentice* but having Chloe as a team leader is very tiring. It makes an hour of Numeracy seem quite relaxing.

We are just packing up to go home when Chloe slides over to me. "Here, put this in your bag," she says, handing me a package.

"What is it?" I ask.

"Card. One hundred sheets."

"But where did you get it?"

"It's mine. I've, er, had it for ages. You know, just hanging around – old arty stuff that I never use. I'm willing to donate it to the cause – *free*. I got my mum to drop it off. I texted her at lunchtime."

"I thought she was travelling, internationally."

"She had the day off. Anyway, your job is to fold it all in half. Tonight."

"That'll take ages!"

"We all have to do our bit, Emily, if we want to win the challenge."

"Yes, but how come the folding is all my bit? What's your bit?"

"We need to play to our strengths, Emily.

116

My strengths are being in charge and getting stuff for free. I have identified your strength as folding," she says, swinging her bag over her shoulder.

"But I—"

"There's no 'I' in team, Emily. See you tomorrow."

CHAPTER 8

Who's the Daddy?

(Mine, unfortunately)

Still Monday

When I get home it is very peaceful. Sabre is asleep on the sofa and Clover is asleep in her buggy, by the living room window. "It's like Sleeping Beauty's castle in here," I say. "Mum, are you here?"

Mum replies from the kitchen, although what she says is not "Hello" – it is more like "*Ommm...*"

 I go through to find her sitting on the kitchen table, cross-legged. "*Ommm ...*" she says again.

"Mum, are you all right?" I say.

"I'm meditating, Emily," she says, without opening her eyes.

"On the table?"

"I tried to do it on the floor but the dog kept jumping on me."

"What's for tea?"

"Sorry, I can't hear you. I am now in a state of complete calm and deep relaxation. The outside world is receding." Then she starts again. "*Ommm ... Ommm ...* Emily, can you get the washing in?"

Hmm. The outside world has obviously not receded far enough for her to forget to give me chores.

I go out into the garden to get the washing. At least it's on the line for once, and not on the clothes airer in the front-room window.

I am just taking down the last pair of socks when I get a funny feeling that someone is watching me. There is no one in the garden, though, and through the kitchen window I can still see Mum on the table with her eyes shut, but I'm definitely getting a creepy feeling again. It must be ...

"Lena! What are you doing there?"

Lena's head is poking through a small hole at the bottom of our hedge.

"Looking for worms," she says. "Or spiders."

"Eww ... why?"

She looks at me and grins. "My mum uses them."

"*Uses* them? What for?"

"Spells," Lena says, in the same way as someone else might say "baking".

Spells! I knew there was something strange about Wanda. And so did Clover – that's why she didn't like her. "Got to go and fold washing," I say. I grab the washing basket and leave Lena staring after me.

"Mum," I say, once I'm back in the kitchen. "Did Wanda teach you all this yoga stuff?"

"*Omm* ..." Mum says, without opening her eyes. Then I think, *What if she's under a spell? What did I say earlier? "It's like Sleeping Beauty's castle ..." What if I was right?*

"Mum! Mum! Wake up!" I grab her by the arm and give her a good shake.

"What the—! Emily, what are you trying to do? You nearly pulled me off the table!"

"Sorry," I say. "I thought you were under a spell."

"What?" Mum takes a deep breath. "Look, Emily, my life is very stressful at the moment. I'm just trying to have a few minutes' peace while the baby is asleep. I'm not under a spell. It's only yoga. It's supposed to be relaxing," she says, her voice getting higher. She makes a big show about doing some deep breathing, closes her eyes again and says, "*Ommm* ..."

At least when she's got her eyes closed I can very quietly get a packet of crisps out of the cupboard without being told it will ruin my tea (which my mum usually does a good job of by herself, anyway). I am just thinking I might go and talk to Bella on the computer and tell her about my new plan to avoid living in an igloo by selling birthday cards, *Oh, and by the way, I have just found out my next-door neighbour is a witch*, when suddenly there is a horrible noise: it is loud and screechy and whiney and seems to be vibrating through the floorboards and up my legs.

Sabre starts howling and, a couple of seconds later, so does Clover.

"Aaaargh! What now?" Mum says, leaping up off the table. The noise seems to be coming from next door. I stick my fingers in my ears but it doesn't really seem to make any difference. Then, as suddenly as it started, it stops. Mum goes into the living room and picks up Clover as she looks out of the window. "What on earth *was* that?" she says. "Oh, hang on. Here comes Dad. I expect he had something to do with it."

The front door opens and Dad comes in, grinning broadly. "Did you hear that?" he says.

"Of course we heard it," Mum says.

"Wasn't it great? It's Griff's new guitar – he was just showing me. Did you know he's a session musician?"

"What's that?" I ask.

"A guitarist who plays for lots of different groups when they record their music. He's met all the greats. He's even met The Megatronics."

"Marvellous," Mum says. "Well, you can tell him if he makes a racket like that again he will also meet the Environmental Health Officer, because that's who I'll be calling." She heads for the stairs, saying, "I'm going upstairs to change Clover's nappy, now that she's awake. As you seem to have finished work early, perhaps you could take the flipping dog for a walk. And, Emily, put those crisps away. They'll ruin your tea."

"I'll walk the dog later," Dad says. "I've promised to go round to Griff's again in a bit, to work on some ideas."

"Ideas for what?" Mum says, stopping halfway up the stairs and turning to face us. "One thousand and one ways to deafen your neighbours?"

"For the disco. After all, I don't want to let Emily down, do I? And Griff is working on something too. Pulling some strings."

"I don't mind him pulling some strings," Mum says. "Just don't let him play any."

"We've got a little surprise planned for the Juniper Road school disco this year," Dad says. He winks at me and follows Mum upstairs.

Oh, great. A surprise. That's the last thing I need. Life with my family is one surprise after another – trouble is, none of them are the good type. We *really* have to win this *Apprentice* competition and get some money to the PTA to get a proper DJ. If we don't, and Dad does it instead, I'll have to go and live in a cave, which doesn't sound like much fun. And, apart from anything else, I've no idea where to find one at short notice.

Thinking that reminds me of all the card that needs folding. I go into the living room and open the package Chloe gave me. One hundred sheets of multi-coloured card. It was very convenient the way she just happened to have some lying around. I make a start with the folding but it's very boring and I have had enough by the time I've done about five.

I am just trying to convince myself that maybe Dad's disco won't be so bad – maybe I can persuade him to play some good music and if I hide in the toilet most of the night people might not even realise we're related – when he comes downstairs again.

"What do you think, Em?" he asks. He is wearing tight white jeans and a purple flowery shirt with the top three buttons undone, showing a gold chain around his neck.

I try to say, "No, Dad! You can't go out like that!" but all that comes out is a sort of high-pitched squeaky sound.

"I know. Cool, right? It's my DJing outfit. Gotta look the part. I was thinking I might do a bit of rapping – you know, something like, *I'm DJ Dad, you know I'm bad / When I play my songs, you've gotta dance along / I play my tracks, turned up to the max / So come on laddie shout, Who's the Daddddddddy!* Ha! What do you think? Well, maybe it needs work. OK, I'm off to see Griff." And he goes off leaving a waft of stinky aftershave behind him.

I start folding cards again as fast as I can.

CHAPTER 9

Wild Card

Tuesday morning

My arms are totally aching this morning after an entire evening of card-folding. Zuzanna is getting a lift in to school so I have to carry the whole load of card in two carrier bags, on my own, which makes my muscles ache even more. By the time I get to school I am sure my arms have stretched so far that I will never look normal again.

To make things worse, Loopy Lena walked behind me all the way but every time I turned around, she pretended to be doing up her shoe or something. I think she's stalking me. At least she could have caught up and offered to carry one of the bags. Although then I would only have one stretched arm and that might look even worse. Zuzanna would probably refuse to be friends with me if I wasn't symmetrical.

I get into class and drop the bags next to our table. Alfie doesn't look very happy, either. Just as we were going home yesterday, Chloe gave him the task of drawing the teapots.

"How many have you done, Alfie?" Chloe says, flicking through the big pile of paper in the middle of the table.

"About fifty," he says. "It takes ages to draw a teapot. Parsnips would have been much easier."

"We will be selling quality, handcrafted goods,

Alfie," Chloe says. "No one expects to see a parsnip on a luxury item."

"But my hand is really aching from all this drawing," he says.

"You have to expect to put a bit of effort in for the team," Chloe says.

"Well, I don't see you putting much effort in," Alfie replies.

"Alfie, Alfie. What you don't understand is that I am a leader. And you are so not. So you'd better start drawing a few more. Like, fifty more."

Amy-Lee comes over to see how we are getting on. "I need to report back to Mrs Lovetofts on any problems within the team," she says. "How are you finding your team leader?"

"Bossy," Alfie says.

"Hmm. I see," Amy-Lee says, and ticks something on her clipboard.

"And how are you getting on with the task?"

"Slowly," I say.

"Hmm. I see," Amy-Lee says, and ticks something else on her clipboard.

"And what about expenses?"

"What about them?" Chloe says. "We don't have any."

"Hmm. I see," Amy-Lee says and does another load of ticking, then goes off. I'm not sure if the ticking is good or bad. To be honest, I don't think Amy-Lee knows either, but at least having both her hands busy means she hasn't given anyone a Chinese burn this morning.

Zuzanna and I start colouring in the teapots and Yasmin is supposed to cut them out, but she keeps cutting off the spouts. Then she gets bored and sneaks up behind Amy-Lee and starts cutting her hair, so we give her the job of making sure none of the other teams spy on us. She sits in a chair and growls if anyone comes too near.

It's a very boring day. Making cards is OK if you

only have to do a couple, but making a hundred all the same is totally not at all interesting.

After we have done all the colouring, cutting out and sticking we have to write "Happy Birthday" across the top of each one. My hand is aching so much I decide to give myself a break and go to see what the other teams are making. Fortunately, they don't have a Yasmin to keep me away.

Team Succeed is making nice gift boxes. "We're going to put chocolates in them," Small Emily B. says.

"Good idea," I say.

Team Achieve has disappeared.

"They're in the kitchen making cookies," Mrs Lovetofts says. "Isn't that a clever idea?"

"Great," I say. I really hope there are a load of tea addicts at the fete tomorrow.

"Aren't you working with your team, Emily?" Mrs Lovetofts says.

"I'm just having a little break, Miss," I say. "I've got total aching hand-itus."

"Well, if you've got a spare minute, perhaps you wouldn't mind popping down to the office to ask Mrs Brace to photocopy this timetable for me," she says, holding out a piece of paper.

I am very glad to have an excuse to get away from teapots for five minutes, so I go down to the office to see Mrs Brace.

"Hello, Emily," Mrs Brace says.

"Could you copy this for Mrs Lovetofts, please?" I ask.

She takes the paper from me as the phone rings. "Just a minute," she says. "I need to get this."

She answers the phone and in a rather stern voice says, "Yes, thanks for calling me back. I want to complain about the craft order that was delivered yesterday. We asked for ten packs of card but only nine arrived." There is a little pause and then she says in an even sterner voice, "And I can assure you, *young man*, that there were only nine. They were in a stack in the reception area and I put them into the stock cupboard myself ... Yes, a £10 refund *would* be in order. Thank you."

She hangs up the phone and gives me a tight little smile. "You can't let them get away with it, Emily. Daylight robbery."

Mrs Brace hands me the photocopied timetable to take back to Mrs Lovetofts. "Are you OK, Emily?" she says.

"Daylight robbery!" I say, and head off back down the corridor.

By the time I get back to the classroom, everyone is clearing up to go home. Our teapot cards are stacked in a box. Zuzanna is just finishing writing "Happy Birthday" on the last few.

"Well done, team," Chloe says, coming back to the table. "I have been looking at the other teams' efforts, and I'm totally sure we are going to win."

"But the others do have good products," Zuzanna says.

"Yes, but think how much money they spent on buying chocolates and baking ingredients. It will all have to come off their profit. Whereas we have managed to make our cards for *free*. Totally, *totalement* free, and with no expenses. That's good team management for you," she says, with a smug grin.

All the time we are packing up to go home, I am feeling ill.

"Chloe," I say, when everyone else is busy. "Can I have a word?"

"Of course, Emily. I operate

an open door style of
management."

"Where exactly did
that card come from?"

"I told you. I found it lying
around."

"Because a pack of card went
missing from outside Mrs Brace's office."

"Really? What a coincidence."

I take a deep breath. "You took it,
didn't you?"

"Emily! I am totally hurt by your
accusation. When have you ever
known me to be dishonest?"

"Well, there was the—"

"No, I'm sorry, I can't discuss it any more.
A team is based on trust, Emily. I think that's
something you need to think about overnight. See
you tomorrow," she says, and walks off.

I look at the cards sitting in a box on the table.

I'm sure it's Mrs Brace's card – it's too much of a coincidence. Of course, I can't prove it and, anyway, it's a bit late to give it back now, but I just can't feel good about these cards.

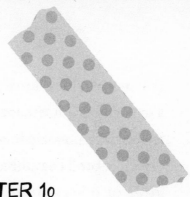

CHAPTER 10

Into the Witch's Den

Tuesday afternoon

Unfortunately, Mum and Wanda seem to be getting on really well. So well, in fact, that they are both outside school waiting for us all to walk back together. I manage to ignore Lena most of the way by getting Zuzanna to talk non-stop about the NV Boyz, but when we reach her house I'm totally stuck with Lena.

We walk along in silence for a bit. I have Sabre on the lead so I pretend to be very involved in training him. "Heel, Sabre," I say, because I have heard loads of other proper dog people saying it, although I'm not really sure what that means. But I'm pretty sure Lena won't know what it means either, because she has a stuffed crow not a dog.

"Barney's OK," Lena says, like she's read my mind. Which she probably has.

I shudder. "What do you mean?"

"After you kicked him."

"I didn't kick him. I tripped over the box."

"It's my dad's hobby, you know."

"What is? Tripping people up?"

"Taxidermy. Stuffing birds and mice and other dead things. He's got loads of them," she says, looking at me out of the corner of her eye.

"Barney is his favourite, though."

"Really?" I say, even though what I really want to say is: "Mum! Why are you making me walk with this weirdo?"

"He found him in the garden. Dead as anything. So he brought him in and stuffed him," she says, with a creepy grin.

And I think, *I'm very glad my Dad's hobby is playing football.*

"Your dog's really small," she says, and glances down at Sabre and I'm sure she's thinking about getting him stuffed, too.

I pull his lead tight and march off ahead. "Got homework to do – see you later," I say. "Come on, Sabre. Totally heel now."

A bit later Gran comes round. She is very pleased because she has bought me a present.

"A new dress, Emily. I heard there's a disco coming up and I thought this would be just the thing."

Actually, for my gran, it is not a bad choice. It is pink, which is not great, and it is a size too small because she always forgets how old I am, but it is quite fashionable and at least she didn't knit it herself.

"Thanks, Gran," I say, and Mum smiles at me, although we both know that I will never wear it. I leave them chatting because it's very boring listening to Gran telling Mum about her exciting new recipe for cauliflower cheese, and also because I don't want her to ask me what I did at school today, because I don't even want to think about teapot birthday cards any more. I'm pretty sure I will be dreaming about them until the fete anyway.

Sabre is in the kitchen looking miserable, as usual. I should take him out for a walk but I am not feeling up to meeting everyone in the street and saying "Hello", and admiring their poo bags. I am too tired from card-making. I let Sabre out into the back garden to walk himself.

A few minutes later the phone rings. Mum and Gran are still deep in natter-ation so, as usual, I have to answer it.

There is a very strange noise on the other end, like: "*Mubbbbbbbb, mubbb.*"

"Hello?" I say.

There is a loud snorty, sniffy noise. "It's Daidy."

"Daidy? Oh, Daisy. Are you OK?" Oh, no. I hope she and Uncle Clive haven't broken up. I am not giving up my bedroom again.

"Just calling to see how S-S-Sabre is. *Bwwwwwaaah.*"

There is a bit of rustling and then Uncle Clive

comes on the phone. "Hi, Emily. Daisy is really missing Sabre. In fact, we've decided to come back a bit early. Would it be OK if we picked him up this evening?"

"Oh! Yes, fine." I will be sorry to see Sabre go, but not too sorry. Looking after a dog is harder than you'd think.

"See you in an hour or so then," Uncle Clive says.

I go out into the back garden to get Sabre; I'd better make sure he's had a bit of a clean-up and brush before Daisy comes.

"Sabre," I call. "Sabre, come on!" But Sabre doesn't come. I look around the garden. "Sabre! Where are you?" He must be here somewhere. "Sabre?"

I start to feel a bit panicky. But I tell myself there is nowhere he could have gone: the gate to the front is shut, and there's a wall on one side of the garden and a hedge between us and the Izzards.

I walk around the garden once more looking under bushes and behind pots. And then I see it: the hole under the hedge where Lena was collecting spiders. There are some little doggy footprints in the mud. He must have gone through to the Izzards' garden. I get down on the ground and look through the hole in the hedge. Yes, there he is, near their back door, which is wide open.

"Sabre!" I hiss. "Sabre, come here!"

But he doesn't come; he just sits down on the path.

"Sabre, will you please just come?"

Of course I could just go round and knock on the Izzards' door and ask them to bring him back.

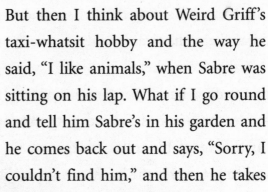

But then I think about Weird Griff's taxi-whatsit hobby and the way he said, "I like animals," when Sabre was sitting on his lap. What if I go round and tell him Sabre's in his garden and he comes back out and says, "Sorry, I couldn't find him," and then he takes him and ... No! I can't even think it.

But then, what if I go into the garden to get him and Wanda catches me? She might turn me into a frog or something. Then Griff might taxi-whatsit *me*!

"Sabre. Pleeeeeease!"

Sabre looks at me and wags his tail.

There's nothing for it – I'll have to go through and get him. I stick my head further through the gap. There's no one around. I lie on my belly and wriggle my way through the gap, getting mud all over my school clothes and leaves in my hair. At last, scratched and dirty, I get through.

146

Sabre is still sitting in the same place and I crawl down the path towards him.

"Sabre, come here," I whisper, keeping one eye on the open back door. Sabre stands up and looks at me; then, just as I'm reaching out my hand to catch hold of his collar, he turns and runs towards the house.

Straight in through the Izzards' back door.

Disaster! Now what? Daisy will be here in half an hour and I'll have to explain her dog has been kidnapped by a witch and a taxi-whatsit man! I creep down the path until I am right beside the back door, crouch down with my back to the wall, and listen. It seems to be all quiet inside. I cross both my fingers and peer round the door into the kitchen.

Sabre is sitting in the middle of the floor looking at me. If I didn't know better I'd think he was grinning.

"Sabre! Come here!" I hiss. I take one last look around and crawl through the door and across the tiles towards him. My heart is pounding and my hands are all tingly and sweaty, but I reach out slowly and manage to catch hold of Sabre's collar. Then I freeze. There is a sound. Sort of familiar – kind of like a little xylophone being played. Coming from somewhere in the kitchen.

I have a nanosecond thinking there must be a small musician sitting on the fridge but then realise it is coming from a mobile phone on the kitchen worktop. And then I think, *If there's a phone ringing, someone is going to come and answer it.* I grab Sabre and do a sort of commando roll under the kitchen table, which is very impressive, actually, but I don't have time to feel pleased with myself as the door opens and a pair of purple-velvet-covered legs strolls past us.

My heart is thumping so hard that I am sure Weird Griff can hear it.

"Hi!" he says and I think, *That's it. He's found me. We're doomed.* But then I realise he's not talking to me. He's answered the mobile.

"Yes, fine … You got them? The Megatronics playing live? … That's fantastic! My mate, Keith, will be so pleased. And what time will the lads be turning up tomorrow? … 7.30 p.m. Perfect. This is one school disco the kids are not going to forget. I owe you one, mate," he says, as he walks out of the kitchen.

The Megatronics. At the school disco! Dad said

Griff was working on a surprise. A bunch of hairy old rockers playing screechy guitars.

The surprise will be if I am ever allowed to set foot in my school again.

 So now I am covered in mud and leaves, hiding from a witch and her husband, under a table, clutching a very small, shaking dog. Really, things couldn't get any worse.

The kitchen door opens and a familiar pair of clumpy black shoes attached to skinny black legs walks past.

OK. Things *could* get worse.

Sabre wriggles to get free. I am sure any minute now he's going to bark. I hear Lena turn on the tap and fill a glass of water. And then I hear something else. A kind of sniffy, blubby sound. Just like I heard Daisy make half an hour ago. Lena is crying. She blows her nose and sniffs some more and then (thank you Wavey Cat, Fairy Godmother, Gok Wan or anyone else who is helping out), she walks back out of the kitchen.

I scramble out from under the table, dragging Sabre with me, and bolt out of the door and down the garden path.

Somehow I manage to get back through the hedge with Sabre under my arm and burst into our kitchen in a breathless panic.

"Emily! What on earth?" Mum has a total freak-out about the state of my school clothes and my hair, and the dog. Then Dad phones and says he has to work late and she does a bit more freaking out. I have to spend half an hour looking after Clover while she goes to meditate to calm down.

I tell Clover all about the disco disaster while I am brushing Sabre.

"And now The Megatronics are going to play," I say.

"Yaaaaaaaa," Clover screeches, which is quite a good impression.

I have only just finished getting all the mud and leaves out of Sabre's fur when Daisy and Uncle Clive turn up.

"Has he been a good boy?" Daisy asks, tears running down her cheeks.

"Perfect," Mum says, walking into the living room. "Hasn't he, Emily?"

"Oh, yes," I say. "He's been great."

Emily says: Bella. Things are getting worse.

Bella says: Worse? Wow. Is that possible?

Emily says: Dad has got some ancient old rock band coming to play at the school disco as well. And he's going to do a rap.

Bella says: Wow. It is possible.

Emily says: And Mum is trying to make me be friends with the weird girl next door.

Bella says: Perhaps she's not as weird as you think.

Emily says: She wears black eyeliner and massive shoes and doesn't talk to anyone.

Bella says: Nice people can wear eyeliner. Maybe she's just a bit different.

Emily says: It doesn't matter because after the disco I'm not going to have any friends either. I'm moving to the Arctic.

Bella says: You can come and live with us. Wales is a bit damp, but goats are a lot less scary than polar bears.

🐰 Emily says: My only hope is to sell 100 cards with teapots on.

🐶 Bella says: Start packing now.

I go up to my room to see Wavey Cat.

"Wavey Cat. Please – you are not doing what you're supposed to do. When I said we need a disco with really good music, I meant music that people my age think is good. Not people from ancient times. Perhaps I wasn't being clear enough. Or maybe you just have rubbish taste in music, like my Dad and Weird Griff. Anyway, please can you make an effort," I say, flicking his paw. "After all, that's why I employ you." I am not usually so bossy with Wavey Cat. Maybe it comes from spending so much time with Chloe.

I turn around and step on a wet patch on the carpet.

A goodbye present from Sabre.

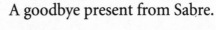

CHAPTER 11

Time to Put the Cards on the Table

Wednesday

We are sitting on the ENDSHIP SEA after lunch.
I am trying not to look over at the field where
my mum is doing the Allotment Club in her
scarecrow clothes. But, to be honest, not
even that is bothering me much
any more. Friday's looming

disaster is sort of blotting out all the other disasters in my life.

This morning I had to walk to school with Lena the Lizard again. She still has her black nail varnish on. It's really  unfair that she doesn't get told off. Mum says they're probably letting her settle in after she was bullied in her last school. I'm not sure I believe all that about her being bullied, anyway: she's the scary one. She probably got made to leave for creeping people out with her black-eyed zombie stare.

Zuzanna and Chloe are talking about the disco – for a change.

"It's going to be great. I really love it when they have all that disco lighting and stuff. DJ Derek Diamond is really good, isn't he?" Zuzanna says.

"It might not be DJ Derek Diamond," I say.

"Of course it is. Who else would it be?" Zuzanna says.

"Well, we've got to get this school fete out of the way before we think about anything else," I say, trying to change the subject.

"Oh, sorry, team. I forgot to mention I won't be here this afternoon," Chloe says.

"What?"

"I've got a dentist appointment. My mum is picking me up."

"But what about the fete?" I say.

"You two will be fine. And you've got Alfie and Yasmin to help. You need to take responsibility now – I've done as much as I can to pass on my business knowledge. Team *Oui* is all yours. Take this baby and make her fly!"

"But, Chloe—!" I say as the bell goes for the end of lunch.

159

"Gotta go," she says, picking up her school bag. She heads across the playground while we watch her in amazement. Just as she gets to the door she turns back to wave. "Go *Oui*! Go *Oui*!" she shouts, and she disappears into school.

By the time we get into class Chloe has gone, but there is no time to worry as Mrs Lovetofts is making a big fuss about everyone going through to the hall with their "amazing products".

"You only have two hours," she says, "so make sure you sell, sell, sell!"

We have been given a table and a tin to put the money in. It is a very big, empty-looking table and a very big, empty-looking tin.

Everyone else is setting up their tables too. Gracie McKenzie's mum is doing the "Guess How Many Sweets in the Jar" competition. There are 347. Gracie told me but I'm not going to have a go because I don't like mint imperials.

Yeah-Yeah Yasmin's mum is doing nails. You can have them painted with zebra stripes or have little diamonds stuck on the end. I think, *That would be good for Alfie – it might stop him picking his nose.*

Mrs Lovetofts is running a big tombola next to our table. It has a tin of carrots, some dried peas, a can of pilchards and about a million other things that no one would ever want to win. Except there is one big box of chocolates, right in the middle of the table. They had to put that in or no one would buy a ticket.

"We need to make a sign," Zuzanna says. "Chloe says it should attract customers with our USP."

"Our what?"

"Our USP – unique selling point. The thing that makes our product different from anyone else's."

"Which is what?"

"Well, I'm not sure. Chloe didn't say."

Zuzanna and I spend a few minutes thinking about what is unique about our cards. Mainly I think it is that our cards are more rubbish than 99 per cent of other cards you can buy. But I don't want to be negative. "I suppose our USP could be teapots. No one else here is selling cards with teapots on."

"No, but someone else is selling cards. Look!" Zuzanna says.

On the other side of the hall a woman is arranging her table. She

162

has loads of brightly coloured cards with lots of different designs. She puts up a big sign which says:

Crafty Cards - Beautiful Handmade Greeting Cards

Some of the teachers are already looking at her stall and the fete hasn't even started yet.

"That's not fair," I say. "She's not even a parent, is she?"

"She's better than that," Zuzanna says. "She's Mr Meakin's wife."

I wander over to look at her stall. She looks exactly like you would expect Mr Meakin's wife to look, with a flowery scarf and too much orange lipstick.

"Hello, dear," she says. "I see you two little girls are selling cards, too."

"Yes," I say. "We're raising money for the dis— I mean, for the PTA."

"Oh, yes. I will be making a donation to the school, of course. I understand my husband could do with a new scarf."

"Is that a donation to the school, then?"

"Of course it is," she snaps. "Essential, work-related clothing. He can hardly supervise rugby practice without a scarf."

"You have got an awful lot of cards," I say, picking up one with a glittery butterfly design.

"Don't touch, dear," she says, snatching it out of my hand.

"Do you make them all yourself?" I ask.

"Oh, yes. If you want to be successful, you have

to put the work in. Something you youngsters need to learn, I'm afraid. Still, never mind – I'm sure your mum will buy one of yours."

Back at the stall I tell Zuzanna about Mrs Meakin.

"Don't worry," Zuzanna says. "If she gets too popular we'll send our secret weapon in."

"What's that?"

"We'll get Alfie to go and stand by her stall. That'll put most of the customers off."

Alfie seems quite pleased by this idea and shows it by doing an especially musical burp.

 Yasmin comes over and says, "Can't help you lot 'cos I've got to help my mum do nails. She's rubbish at ladybird spots."

Alfie seems to have drifted off too, probably to find Gross-Out and plan something disgusting. We don't bother trying to get him back: burps never attract customers, even musical ones. So that just leaves me and Zuzanna and a pile of cards.

We decide to write "Utterly Unique Birthday Greetings – Handmade Cards" on the sign. Zuzanna does it in posh writing and we prop it up on the table.

At 2.30 p.m. they open the doors to let everyone in. Mr Meakin stands on the stage and says, "Good afternoon, ladies and gentlemen, and parents." He gives a little speech about what a great fete it will be and how there are many lovely stalls. "We have a raffle, a tombola and our special stalls from

Year Six's *Apprentice* competition. There are chocolates from Team Success—"

"Succeed," Small Emily B. calls.

"And cookies are available from Team Believe," he continues.

"Achieve!" Joshua says.

"And, of course, you can get lovely birthday cards from ... my wife."

"He didn't even mention us!" Zuzanna says.

"And can I just mention, if anyone finds a woolly scarf, I would be grateful if they would hand it in to me. Oh, yes – I declare this fete open!"

Most people stopped listening at "Good afternoon", and they're all nosing around the stalls. Mrs Meakin has a queue already, and there are a lot of pensioners hanging around the mint imperials.

We sell four cards in the first couple of minutes: two to Zuzanna's mum, who is supposed to be helping out on the cake stall but seems to have

167

escaped already, and two to my mum who, very embarrassingly, has decided to come to the fete in her gardening clothes with actual mud on her nose. Then it goes a bit quiet until Gran turns up.

"Oh, *look* at these. Marvellous!" she says. "Teapots! Genius idea. I'll have five." She starts rounding up her friends. "Look over here, Mrs O'Leary. Did you ever see such a lovely display? My granddaughter. Isn't she talented? You need to buy some. Now."

Mrs O'Leary doesn't look very convinced but buys one card as Gran goes off in search of other victims – I mean, customers. A few minutes later I spot her dragging a very elderly man by the elbow away from Mrs Meakin's stall.

"Now then," she says. "Aren't these cards much better, Mr Cornthwaite? He'll take three, Emily."

While Mr Cornthwaite is counting out his money Gran nabs another customer. "And Mrs Larsson? You don't want any? Funny, I was thinking about you just the other day and that incident in 1982 with the waiter at the community centre Christmas party. That's right, I still remember it all like yesterday ... oh good, you've changed your mind. Another three cards for Mrs Larsson, Emily. Oh, look, there's Mrs Lewis – she owes me one for covering up when she double-booked the Pensioners' Pilates with the Ultra Zumba Club. Yoo-hoo! Mrs Lewis!"

While Mrs Lewis is buying her cards, Gran goes over to see the cards on Mrs Meakin's stall. I'm sure it was just bad luck that Mrs Meakin's table collapsed while Gran was looking at her display; however, a couple of minutes later, Mr Meakin arrives and asks if he can have a quiet word with Gran before guiding her away by the elbow.

Without Gran's help our stream of customers dries up: by 3.30 p.m. we have still only sold eighteen cards. We try rearranging them and propping our sign up higher, but it's no use. We have to face it. We are not going to sell any more cards unless it's through sympathy or blackmail.

"You may as well have a look around the fete if you want to, Zuzanna," I say. "I can manage on my own for a bit. Well, completely, really. In fact, we could probably leave the stall altogether for all the difference it makes."

"I don't have any money," Zuzanna says. "You look around if you want."

"I only have one pound."

"You could buy a couple of cards."

"I don't think there's much point in buying any. We'd still have eighty spare ones in an hour's time."

I look around the fete. I really don't want to buy anything. By the time you get to Year Six, school fetes have lost their appeal. There are only so many times you can get excited about guessing the name of the teddy bear or not making the wire thing go buzz. Team Succeed have nearly sold out of chocolates. And Team Achieve have already closed their stall as they've sold all their biscuits.

My sliver of hope is heading for the door again.

The Year Five girls are taking it in turns to run the face-painting stall. I'm surprised to see Lena is joining in, although she still looks pretty miserable. She is painting whiskers on a little kid who wants to be a cat.

A couple of Year Five boys are giggling. "Hey," one of them says, "don't let her do it or everyone will look like a lizard!" They burst out with snorty laughter.

Lena shoves the face-painting tray back at one of the girls. "I hate this stupid school," she says, and runs off.

"That wasn't very nice," the girl says to the boys. "It took me ages to persuade her to join in."

"It's not our fault she's weird, is it?" the boy says.

I think about going after Lena and making sure she's OK. But then I think if she's going to go around saying she hates this school all the time, she can't expect people to like her. I mean, there's not a lot I can do if she's going to have that sort of attitude ... is there? I decide to forget about Lena and get on with enjoying the fete. I'm going to spend my money on the tombola – at least there's a chance of winning the box of chocolates, which is still in pride of place in the middle of the table. I get five tickets for my £1.

"If they end with a zero or a five you've won a prize," Mrs Lovetofts says.

I pick out five tickets from a basket and open them one by one. With my usual luck I get nothing from the first four tickets. I am not expecting anything from my fifth ticket, either, but when I open it I am surprised to see it is 120.

"Oh! I won! I won a prize," I say excitedly.

Mrs Lovetofts takes the ticket from me. "Yes, indeed. You have," she says. "Now then, let me see." She scans the tickets on the prizes. Unfortunately, she passes straight over the box of chocolates and starts rummaging around in the tins of beans and custard powder section. "Here we go, Emily. You've won … a box of eighty individually wrapped teabags!"

I cannot even bring myself to say thank

you. Teabags. It is like someone is playing a bad joke on me, and I can't help wondering if I was wrong to be so bossy to Wavey Cat.

"Teabags?" Zuzanna says, when I get back to the table. "Great, just what we need to go with our teapots."

And then – finally – I have a flash of Emily Sparkes creativityness.

"Zuzanna, I've got an idea!" I say. "Get your best pens out – we've got some work to do! I've found us our USP!"

Fifteen minutes later, we have a queue and Mrs Meakin is looking across the hall with folded arms and tightly pursed orange lips.

We have written our sign again: *Unique Birthday Cuppa Gift Cards*. At the bottom of every card, underneath the teapot, Zuzanna has written: Relax. Have a Cup of Tea on Me! and inside each card I have stuck a teabag.

"Give your friends a little tea break!" I call. "Unique cards that everyone will appreciate."

We are serving customers as fast as we can. Our tin is filling up with coins.

"Great idea, Emily," Mum says, appearing at the front of the queue. "I'll take some for Gran."

"Where *is* Gran?" I say.

"I think she and Mr Meakin came to a mutual agreement," Mum says.

"What does that mean?"

"She could either leave quietly or pay for all the squashed cards on the Crafty Cards stall. It's just like the Christmas cake at the carol service all over again." She sighs.

{175}

"Aren't they marvellous? Such a clever idea," Mrs Lovetofts says, bounding over. "I'm very proud of my little *Oui*s."

"I beg your pardon?" Mum says.

"Do you have any of those with herbal teabags?" asks Wanda Izzard, appearing behind Mum.

"Er … no," I say, hoping she doesn't put a curse on me.

"Oh, yes, we can!" Mrs Lovetofts says. "Give me a minute." She rushes off and comes back a couple of minutes later with a tatty box in her hand. "Liquorice and camomile?" she says.

"Lovely," says Wanda.

"They've been in the staffroom cupboard for years," Mrs Lovetofts whispers to me and Zuzanna, as Wanda counts out her change.

By 4.30 p.m. we have completely sold out and

we are completely exhausted. But I still manage to summon up enough energy to count the takings. Exactly £50. We must be in with a good chance of winning.

"So, do you think we won the challenge?" says a girl standing next to me.

"Sorry?" I turn to look at her properly.

"I am so looking forward to Mrs Lovetofts saying, 'You're hired, Chloe.' We had a much better business model than the others, don't you think?"

"Chloe! What are you doing here? And hang on, have you had your hair cut?"

"Yes. I thought it was more business-like."

"But you said you were going to the dentist!"

"The dentist was really quick, so I thought I might as well get my hair done, too."

"But you could have come back to help us," Zuzanna says. "Do you know how hard we've been working?"

"I know. I really wanted my hair done tomorrow morning, before the boardroom, but the hairdressers refuse to open before nine. I told them that's no way to run a business. Still, I knew you'd want me to get it done. It's so important to our success that the team leader presents the right image."

"It's also important to sell some stuff, Chloe."

"So, come on. How much did we make?"

"*We* made £50," I say.

"Hmm, not bad."

"Not bad! We worked really hard. We sold everything!"

"Good," Chloe says. "And some more good news. I've decided what to wear to the disco. It's a business suit – you know, with padded shoulders. Bought it this afternoon. *Très chic.*"

"Fantastic," I say. "I'm so glad you enjoyed yourself."

"I know. Such a relief to *finally* find something."
She beams.

Mrs Lovetofts claps her hands. "Can I have
your attention, Year Six?" she says, and everyone
gathers round. "I just wanted to say well done!
Tomorrow morning you can all return to the
boardroom to see who's hired and who's ...
actually, I don't really like that other word
because you've all done so well, so we will just see
who's hired!"

CHAPTER 12

You're Hired!

Thursday

When Zuzanna and I get into class on Thursday, Mrs Lovetofts has already turned it into the boardroom again.

Chloe is standing in front of our table waiting for us. She is wearing her business suit jacket and a pair of steel-rimmed glasses.

"Did you go to the optician, too?" I ask.

"Don't be silly, Emily. These are just plain glass. They're part of my executive image. I need to look the part when I'm hired and presented with the Juniper Road Primary School Young Business Person of the Year Certificate."

"But you don't know you're going to be hired yet."

"Ah! But I do. I've been doing some digging around and I found out which team made the most money."

"Digging around?"

"Yes, I told Gross-Out that if he didn't tell me I'd speak to Mr Meakin about where his favourite woolly scarf went and what exactly is blocking the toilet in the boys' cloakroom."

"Ewww! So, what did he say?" I ask. Even though I know I shouldn't join in with Chloe's scheming, I am desperate to know.

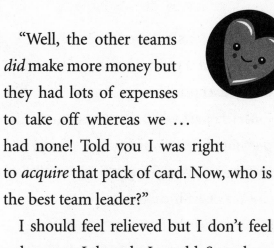

"Well, the other teams *did* make more money but they had lots of expenses to take off whereas we ... had none! Told you I was right to *acquire* that pack of card. Now, who is the best team leader?"

I should feel relieved but I don't feel as happy as I thought I would. Somehow winning by stealing doesn't feel at all nice.

"Sit in your teams, please," Mrs Lovetofts says as she comes in. "It's time for the results."

Gross-Out and Amy-Lee sit either side of Mrs Lovetofts, looking as if they are considerably more important than the rest of us. I notice Amy-Lee has put a ribbon in her hair today. It must feel very out of place.

Mrs Lovetofts seems to have given up on the "*Dum dee-dum dee-dum dee-dum*" and the satsuma voice; it must be hard to be Lord Sugar for a whole week. However, she does say, "Welcome to the boardroom," which actually makes me feel a bit nervous, even though it's only my teacher.

When everyone has settled down Mrs Lovetofts says, "Now for the results. Team Succeed, how was your team leader?"

"She was great," Babette says. "She had really good ideas and spent hours wrapping the chocolates and tying ribbons."

Small Emily B. goes a bit pink. "It was a team effort," she says.

"Yes," Daniel Waller says. "Small Emily B. will probably be an entrepreneur one day."

"Thanks," Small Emily B. says, "but I was really hoping to be a dog groomer."

Mrs Lovetofts turns to her right. "Amy-Lee, can you please give me the all-important figure for Team Succeed."

"Team Succeed sold boxes of chocolates and they made £75."

"Very good," Mrs Lovetofts says.

"But they had expenses of £25.50, so their total profit was ..." Amy-Lee pulls a face. "I hate maths," she says.

"£49.50," Mrs Lovetofts says. "An excellent result."

"Yes, yes. Booooooooring," Chloe mutters.

"Now, Team Achieve, how was your team leader?"

"Joshua was a fantastic team leader," Nicole says.

"Yes," Gracie says. "He stayed up nearly all night decorating the cookies by hand."

"Get on with it," Chloe says.

"Team Achieve sold cookies and they made £58.60," Gross-Out says.

"That's a fantastic result! They must have been great cookies."

"And their expenses were £15, so a total profit of, er ... £43.60?"

"That was an easy one," Amy-Lee says.

"Ha! Told you we've won!" Chloe says. "I am *so* getting that team leader certificate."

"And now we come to Team *Oui*."

Chloe straightens up, folds her hands on the table in front of her and looks over the top of her glasses.

"So, how was Chloe as a team leader?" Mrs Lovetofts asks.

I don't really trust myself to say anything, so I just pretend my foot is itching and keep quiet.

"She knows lots of business-y words," Zuzanna says.

"She's really good at telling people what to do," Alfie says.

"Yeah," Yasmin says.

"Well, that sounds good," Mrs Lovetofts says. "And how much did this team make, Amy-Lee?"

"Team *Oui* sold 100 cards and made £50. They had no expenses. So, a total profit of ... £50!" Amy-Lee says, sounding very pleased with herself.

"Yes!" Chloe says, jumping up and punching the air. "Go *Oui*! Go *Oui*!"

"Well, congratulations!" Mrs Lovetofts says. "It seems that Team *Oui* has won the challenge."

I look across at Joshua and think of him decorating biscuits all night, and then at Small Emily B., who worked so hard to raise money for her nan's old people's home. They are both looking very disappointed.

And even though I desperately want the money for the disco, winning something by cheating and stealing is just not right.

So I make a decision.

"Excuse me, Lord Lovetofts – I mean, Mrs Lovetofts. We did have one expense – didn't we, Zuzanna?"

Chloe turns sharply and looks at me. "No, we didn't, Emily. I told you. I *found* that pack of card."

"What I was going to say was, I spent one pound on the tombola to get the teabags," I say.

"What?" Chloe says. "I didn't authorise that."

"You weren't there," Zuzanna says. "We had to think outside the box and kick it into a whole new ballpark, didn't we, Emily?"

"Er ... possibly," I say.

"But—" Chloe blusters.

"Oh, right," says Amy-Lee. "Just hang on a minute ... that means Team *Oui* made a profit of £49."

"An excellent result Team *Oui*, but that means the winner of the team leader challenge, and the Juniper Road Primary School Young Business Person of the Year is … Small Emily B.!" Mrs Lovetofts points her finger across the table. "Small Emily B., you're hired!"

CHAPTER 13

Engage Brain
Before Opening Mouth

More Thursday

Chloe is still sulking three hours later. "I can't believe we didn't win. Stupid chocolates in a box – that's such a rubbish idea. And Small Emily B. couldn't make an executive decision if someone made it for her."

We are sitting on the ENDSHIP SEA. I am trying

not to think about the fact that I have just ensured that I will spend the rest of my school career as a laughing stock.

"Well, at least the money is going to a good cause," Zuzanna says. "I don't really mind if it goes to the Silver Years Retirement Home – they probably need it more than the PTA. And, anyway, Kit from the NV Boyz's nan is there. I would have liked that Head Teacher's Certificate, though."

"Can I remind you that giving the money to the PTA was Emily's decision?" Chloe says. "In fact, all the rubbish decisions seem to have been Emily's. Like frittering away our profits on teabags!"

I tune out for a bit as Chloe moans on about how unfair everything is. I look around and see Lena sitting against a wall nearby. She is on her own, reading a book.

She looks up and catches my eye and then looks

down again quickly. Two boys run past her shouting, "Hey! Lizard girl!" and then run off laughing.

Chloe is still droning on. "Do you know how hard it is to be a team leader?" she says. "For a start it is very difficult to grab a pack of card from the corridor and shove it up your cardie without getting spotted."

Zuzanna does a little gasp and Chloe bites her lip.

"Well, I'm even more glad we didn't win now," Zuzanna says.

"Oh, you lot fuss too much. School resources are meant to be used by us. Anyway, I am totally sick of all this *Apprentice* stuff," Chloe says. "I need a new challenge."

"Look," Zuzanna says, nodding in Lena's

direction. "It's your neighbour. Sitting over there, reading. She's on her own again."

"It's hardly surprising, she's so weird," I say. "Why does she dress like that?"

"She's an emo," Chloe says.

"An emu?" I say. "I know she owns a stuffed crow, but I don't think she has feathers herself, Chloe."

"*Emo*, Emily. Oh, I forgot – you know nothing at all about fashion. Emos are sort of artistic types. They go around in black looking miserable."

"Why?"

"Because it's a fashion, I suppose. Or maybe because they really are miserable."

"Oh. Do you think she's miserable, then?"

"Well, of course she is, Emily. Why do you think she follows you around all the time? Little Miss No Mates."

"But I thought she was stalking me. To creep me out."

"Face it, Emily – who would ever want to stalk you?"

Zuzanna looks across to where Lena is sitting. "I think she's lonely," she says. "She probably just needs a friend."

"I remember when I was new," Chloe says. "It's not easy. I mean, *obviously* with my magnetic personality I made lots of friends in no time, but if you don't have my natural sparkle it must be quite tough."

I look over at Lena and she doesn't look quite so scary any more. Perhaps Zuzanna's right. Maybe she's just lonely. "Do you think we should try talking to her on the way home, tonight?" I say.

"I'm going shopping with my mum after school," Zuzanna says, "but I think you should. After all, you are her neighbour."

After school, Mum is waiting for me by the gate, with Wanda, her new best friend. They are basically non-stop nattering about yoga. Mum does manage a quick, "Hello-did-you-have-a-nice-day?" but she doesn't wait for the answer before strolling off ahead with Wanda, saying, "Now, run me through the two-headed llama position again."

Lena is clumping along just behind me in an uncomfortably silent way, and I'm sure I can feel her eyes staring at my back. I know I'm supposed to be making an effort to be her friend, but it's not easy.

After a while I can't stand it any more so I turn around and say, "So, how do you like our school?"

"It's just a school," she says. "They're all the same."

"Oh, but I think ours is quite nice, really," I say, desperately trying to think of something nice I can mention. The best I can come up with is, "The chairs in the library are really comfy."

"Library chairs don't really matter when the school is really unfriendly and full of bullies," she says.

"It is not!" I say. "Well, apart from Amy-Lee Langer, and even she's a bit of a rubbish bully, really."

"So people going around shouting 'lizard girl' is nice, is it? Your school is just like all the others – full of horrible people who say mean things and judge other kids just by the way they look."

"That's so not fair!" I say.

"It's the truth," she says.

"Well, it's your own fault! Everyone would be nice to you if you weren't so ... so freaky!"

"See what I mean?" Lena gives me an angry look and storms off ahead.

So what? I don't care. I mean, it's not as if I didn't do my best, is it? I was trying to start a conversation. And, anyway, it's true. If she wasn't so strange – wearing weird clothes and hiding behind books all the time – then she would make more friends.

When I get home I decide to talk to Clover about it. At least I can rely on her to be supportive.

"The thing is, Clover," I say, as she sits in her bouncy seat kicking her legs, "she *is* just freaky. Someone needed to tell her. Didn't they?"

Clover doesn't reply. She just stops kicking her legs and stares at me.

"I was trying to be nice, honestly, but then it kind of went a bit wrong."

How can a baby look so disappointed in me?

"OK. A lot wrong."

Her expression doesn't change. I wish she wouldn't stare at me like that.

"I suppose it wasn't very kind of me. I just got cross."

Clover's eyes get wider and she pulls a strange face.

"I suppose you think I'm mean, too," I say.

Suddenly there is a very loud windy noise from Clover's bottom. "Baaaaaa," she says.

I think I have got my answer.

CHAPTER 14

{

At Your Style Service

Friday morning

I didn't sleep very well last night. I kept thinking that Clover's right. I didn't need to be so mean. After all, Lena is new and I am her next-door neighbour and I am older than her. I should be helping her out, really. It must be a bit difficult if you've been to lots of schools and you have a weird name and weird clothes and weird parents. And her dad is doing the school disco, so that's not going to win her any friends, either.

In fact, we should probably stick together because after *that* disaster, we'll be living in the same cave.

I have decided to apologise and not get cross or mean again, no matter what she says. I am going to be understanding and supportive. I feel a lot better now I've made the decision. In fact, I am almost looking forward to getting things sorted out, but when Mum and I set off to walk to school, Lena isn't leaning in her usual place.

Wanda sticks her head out of her front door. "Lena's not feeling very well this morning," she says. "She's having a day off."

"Oh, what a pity," Mum says. "Emily will have no one to chat to."

Mum is not very observant.

And then I start to worry. What if she's having a day off because of what I said? What if she thinks I'm a bully? What if she never comes back?

Zuzanna has left especially early so she can spend an extra ten minutes standing outside number 47, Cedar Road: she wants to try to get a blade of grass from the front garden, just in case Kit from the NV Boyz once stepped on it. I have no one to distract me from worrying and I worry all the way to school, and even when I get there I am still worrying so much that I don't notice the person who runs up to me as I go in through the gate until she shrieks, "Hi!" and thrusts a card into my hand.

"Er . . . hi, Chloe."

She grabs my shoulders and does an air kiss either side of my cheeks: "Mwah, mwah!"

"Eww! Chloe, what are you doing?"

"Chloe Clarke, fashion consultant and personal

stylist, at your service," she says, through glossy pink lips.

I look at the card in my hand.

Chloe Clarke.
Professional Fashion Consultant
and Personal Stylist.
No challenge too great. School
discos a speciality.

"What's all this about, Chloe?" I ask, as I follow her into class.

"My new business, of course, darling."

"*Darling?*"

"It's what we say in the fashion world. Everybody is darling."

Zuzanna is already in the classroom, proudly showing off the two blades of grass and a daisy she managed to pick.

"Oooh, good, Zuzanna's here. I must give her my card, too," Chloe says. She hurries over to our table, shoves a card into Zuzanna's hand and does the air kissing thing, which nearly causes Zuzanna to fall backwards over the table.

"I am so glad I reassessed my career choices," Chloe says. "I can't be doing with all that rubbish birthday-card-making stuff. I mean – teapots. Really. They're for grannies. I don't know why I let you talk me into it. Manufacturing is in decline – it's all about service industries these days."

"Chloe, I really don't follow you," I say.

"I should have identified my strengths," she says.

"And what exactly are your strengths?"

"Style, elegance and cutting-edge fashion, darling – I mean, just take what I'm wearing today and compare it to what you have on."

What Chloe is wearing is a school sweatshirt, a black skirt and grey woolly tights. I'm not really getting her point.

"What's the matter with my clothes?"
I ask, looking down at my school
jumper and skirt. "They're the same as
yours."

"They're dull, Emily," Chloe says. "You wear the
same thing every day."

"Well, that's because it's the school uniform."

"Except for the other week, of course, when she
wore a summer dress in almost winter," Zuzanna
says, and pulls a slightly annoyed face.

You'd have thought she'd be over that by
now.

"Exactly. I mean, talk about being last
season." Chloe shakes her head.

"That was an emergency."

"And those socks, darling."

"What's the matter with my socks?" I say.
"Zuzanna's got socks on."

"Yes, but at least hers are white. Yours are sort
of … greenish."

"That's because my mum accidentally put them in the washing with Dad's football shirt."

"You'll never make a fashion statement in socks," Chloe says, smoothing her tights.

If you ask me, grey woolly tights don't often make an appearance in fashion magazines either. But, of course, Chloe doesn't ask me, as she is in full flow.

"So, I'm offering my services. Chloe Clarke, personal fashion and stylist consultant – I mean, a fashion person and consultant stylist ... Anyway, what I mean is, you and Zuzanna can be my first clients. Free, because I need to build my portfolio."

"Build *what*? I thought you'd given up on making stuff."

"It means having a list of clients, so you can show you've got experience. Victoria Beckham is not going to let me give her a fashionable new image if I can't show her samples of my work."

"Victoria Beckham?" Zuzanna says. "Why on earth would she want to be restyled by *you*?"

"Oh, when she was at Mag Hall she was always going on about wanting a new fashion consultant."

"Of course, we should have guessed she was at Mag Hall, too. I suppose she was the singing teacher," Zuzanna says.

"No. Football coach," Chloe says. "She picked up a lot of tips from her husband. Now, let's think about the disco. What are you going to wear?"

"I don't know if I mentioned it, Chloe, but I have a new dress," Zuzanna says. "My mum bought it especially, so I have to wear that."

"Hair?"

"My mum's doing it."

"Make-up?"

"I'm not allowed to wear any."

"Seriously, Zuzanna, you are no fun. You need to get your mum to loosen up a bit. How about you, Emily? What are you wearing?"

"I, er, I haven't decided." And I think, *Oh dear, I totally shouldn't have said that.*

"Excellent." Chloe beams. "And obviously your mum hasn't got a clue about hair, or you wouldn't always have it stuffed up in a scraggy ponytail every day. Congratulations, Emily. You are my first challenge."

"But I don't want to be your challenge."

"Nonsense. You want to look good at the disco, don't you?"

Not really, I think, *because I'm not even going to be there.* "Actually, I have a feeling I'm going to be ill tonight," I say. "Or possibly in the Arctic."

Before I have a chance to argue any more, Mrs Lovetofts bustles in with her big flouncy skirt and her hair coming out of her hairclips, as usual. "Hello, my lovely Year Sixes," she says.

"Now there's a challenge for you," Zuzanna mutters to Chloe.

"Darling, some things are too big a challenge even for me," Chloe says.

It has seemed a bit odd at school today without Lena. I am getting used to seeing her sitting around, looking miserable. Now I feel guilty that she's not – if you see what I mean. However, the one good thing about Chloe's fashion consultant thing has been that it has kept me so busy I haven't had time to worry much about the school disco or Lena: I have mostly been kept busy apologising to people who Chloe has just insulted. Like, at breaktime, when Joshua walked past, and she stuck a card in his hand and said, "Hi. Chloe personal Clarke consultant. Do you realise your school trousers are about five centimetres too short, darling?"

Joshua went very pink, although I don't know if that was because of his trousers or because Chloe called him "darling". Good job she didn't do the air kissing thing, or he might have actually fainted.

"Mum says it's because I keep growing," he said.

"Well, give her my card and tell her I said she needs to get you a new pair. No need to be a fashion slouch just because you're a boy."

Next it was Babette's turn. "Hi, Chloe consultant fashion Clarke. Take my card. I couldn't help noticing your shoes. They're really nice."

"Oh, thanks," Babette said. "They're French."

"Ahh, yes, France. The home of style and fashion," Chloe said. "I have a lot of French clothes myself."

"Do you have designer clothes, then?" Babette asked.

"Oh, yes. Mine are mostly Channel."

"It's *Chanel*, not Channel."

Chloe looked a bit annoyed and said, "No, not *Chanel*. That's so last year. Channel is a new designer – Channel, er … Tunnel. She's going to be huge."

"I don't believe you," Babette said. "You're making it up."

"Well, anyway, as I said, nice shoes, darling. Pity your feet are so big," Chloe said. "Got to go. More clients to advise."

Next she told Small Emily B. that blue was totally not her colour and she should consider changing schools to one with a red uniform. Then she told Alfie that he needed a haircut that didn't look like it had been done by his mum with a bowl and her kitchen scissors. Finally, she told Amy-Lee that she should try some Japanese tea because it's good for getting rid of spots. Amy said if Chloe didn't go away she'd try some Chinese burns because they are good for getting rid of fashion consultants.

My face is aching from the apologetic grin I have worn all day.

"Well," Chloe says, as we pack up for the day, "I think that was a rather successful start to my new project. But now for the real challenge. What time shall I come round tonight?"

"Come round?"

"Yes. To help you get ready for the disco."

"What? I don't need help."

"Of course you do, Emily. We've already established you have no idea what to wear and are hopeless at hairstyles. The disco starts at 7 p.m. and I have to get back to get ready myself, so if I pop round at 4 p.m. that should give us plenty of time."

"All right if I tag along, too?" Zuzanna says. "I could do with a laugh – I mean, I could do with getting some fashion ideas."

"But I don't think I'm going to the disco. I feel really ill," I say, which is true, for lots of reasons.

But, as usual, Chloe isn't listening. "See you later," she says. "Must just dash after Gracie and tell her she needs to do something about her coat."

CHAPTER 15

Friend or Freak?

 *Friday afternoon*

I am not going to the disco. I can't face it. I know
Dad has tried his best, but I also know it's going to
be a complete disaster and I will never be able to
hold my head up in public again. I have told Mum
I feel sick and I have a headache and I also said my
legs ache, in case she comes up with some magic
anti-sickness-headache medicine.

Mum says, "I hope you start feeling better soon, Emily. It will be a pity for you to miss the disco."

Dad and Weird Griff have already left for school in Dad's Leaks R Us van, to get the disco set up.

"I'm too ill," I say. "I think I'm getting a cold."

"Your dad has put a lot of effort into this for you and your friends, and you really should go and support him," she says.

"Also my tooth hurts, and I've got a bad back. It could be plague," I say.

She shakes her head at me. "Go and get the washing in and have a think about it," she says, handing me the washing basket.

I don't see how getting the washing in helps you think about anything. That's just an excuse to make me do some housework, but I head off down the garden anyway.

As I am unpegging a pair of leggings I hear a sound. I automatically look towards the hole in the hedge but

there's no one there. I carry on taking
down the washing and then I hear it
again. A sort of sniffy, snuffly sound.
It's coming from the other side of the
hedge.

I try to ignore it, but it happens again and
I think I know what it is, because I've heard it
before. I get down on my hands and knees and
peer through the hole.

Lena is sitting on an upturned flowerpot leaning
against the shed in her garden. She is definitely
crying.

I think about sneaking off again but then I
remember I have made a decision to try to be nice
to her. I wiggle through the hole and pop out the
other side. "Lena? Are you OK?"

She looks up. Her face is all streaky with runny
eyeliner.

"What do you care?"

"Look. Can we try to be friends, Lena?"

She turns her face away. "Call me Lizard." She sniffs. "Everyone else does."

"Not everyone."

"Oh, no. Some people call me 'Weirdo' and 'Loopy Lena', and even 'Freaky'."

I bite my lip. "I'm sorry I was mean. I just got cross when you said you didn't like my school."

Lena sighs. "It's not just your school. This is the third school I've been to and everyone thinks the same."

I go to sit next to her. "But sometimes you act like you don't want to talk to anyone. If you sit in the playground with a book in front of your face, everyone thinks you want to be on your own."

"Good. I'm better off on my own because then no one can say mean things to me."

"And you wear weird clothes and make-up, so people think you're a bit ..."

"Strange? Well, that's good too, because I am."

"Perhaps you should give people a chance. They might like you if you let them."

"There's no point in giving them a chance. They'll just pick on me. I'd rather they just thought I was a scary lizard girl and left me alone."

"So, I guess you're not going to the disco, then?"

"I'm not the sort of girl who goes to school discos. Lizard girls don't have fun. Anyway, I haven't got anyone to go with, have I?"

"I'm not going, either," I say.

She does another little sob. "I just feel bad for my dad, though. He'll be really disappointed. He's been trying so hard to make it fun. He really wants me to get on in this school."

Which makes me think of my dad again, and how hard he's tried to get the disco together, just to make me happy. Mum's right, of course. I should go and support him.

And then I think that Dad and  Lena are a bit the same really – they both need my support, but instead I have been acting like it's embarrassing to be seen with them.

I take a deep breath. "Shall we go together?" I say.

"You don't mean that. You don't really want to go with me."

And I think, *You're right. I don't really want to go with you. In fact, I don't want to go at all. I am just trying to do the right thing.*

"Of course I do," I say. "We're neighbours, right? We share the same hole in the hedge."

"Really?" Lena looks up like she thinks maybe I'm having a joke.

"Really," I say.

She goes quiet for a moment like she's trying to decide if she can trust me. "I suppose we could go," she says slowly. "Dad would be so pleased."

"So would mine," I say.

"So ..."

"So, let's go disco!" I say in the most enthusiastic way I can manage.

And, for the first time, I see Lena smile. Properly smile, not just a shifty grin, and it makes her look different – kinder and prettier.

"OK. Cool. But I'd better go and check with my mum. Come on."

She gets up off the flowerpot and starts walking towards her house.

I hesitate. Lena's house is not somewhere I want to go unless I really have to. "I'll wait here," I say.

"I need you to help me choose what to wear, though. It won't take long."

I can't think of another excuse so I follow her in, but I leave the door open in case I need to make an emergency exit.

The kitchen, which looks quite different when

you are standing up in it, and the living room, are very normal. There are no broomsticks or cauldrons anywhere.

"Mum?" calls Lena.

"In the back room," her mum answers. "I'm meditating. *Ommm* ... "

"Sounds familiar," I say.

"I'm going to the disco, Mum. With Emily," Lena says, and smiles at me.

"Really?" says her mum. "That's great. *Ommm.* I'll give you a lift. *Ommm.*"

We head for the stairs, passing another room. "My dad's special room," Lena says, opening the door to show me.

"I don't really know if I want to—" I start to say, imagining hundreds of tiny glass eyes staring at me.

"It's his music room," Lena says.

I peer cautiously through the door. There are three guitars propped up against the wall, an electric keyboard and a music system. There are also hundreds of LPs, just like Dad's, lining the walls.

Apart from Barney, sitting on a shelf, there is no sign of any stuffed animals or any glassy eyes.

"Where does he keep all his taxi-whatsit stuff?" I whisper.

"Oh, right. About that ..." She looks at the floor.

I look at her. "Your dad isn't a taxi-thingy, is he?"

"No. He loves animals. He's a vegetarian. Well, except for bacon sandwiches."

"But what about Barney?"

"Dad found him in a skip and felt sorry for him."

"And your mum's not a witch."

Lena bites her lip. "You didn't really believe that, did you?"

"Well ... I ... No, of course not. But why did you say all that stuff?"

"I don't know. You were being mean to me so I thought I'd get you back. Sorry."

"It's OK. But if we're going to be friends, no more stuff like that, right?"

"OK. I won't mention that my uncle's a vampire, then." She laughs, and heads upstairs.

I'm pretty sure she's joking.

We look through Lena's clothes. They are mostly black and not at all disco-ish. Lena frowns. "I don't know what to wear to a disco," she says. "What about this?" She holds up a longish black dress with fishnet sleeves.

"It's OK," I say, "but if you want to stop people thinking you're strange, then maybe you should dress in a more ... ordinary way."

"Do you think that will make a difference? I don't really have any ordinary clothes. What are you wearing?" she says.

"Well, I've got a T-shirt with a picture of a dream-catcher on the front. I really like it, but I've got a feeling Chloe's going to have other ideas. Oh no!" I gasp. "Chloe! I forgot all about her."

"Who?"

"What's the time?"

"Er ... five to four."

And then I get a very good idea. "On second thoughts, it might be just what you need. In fact, you might be doing me a big favour, too."

"What do you mean?"

"You'll see ..."

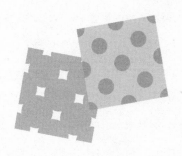

CHAPTER 16

Fashion Victims

More Friday afternoon

We get back to my house just as the doorbell rings.

"Chloe? What *are* you wearing?" I ask, as she marches past me in a white doctor's coat.

"It's my consultant's jacket, darling. Zuzanna, my new assistant, has my toolkit," Chloe says, waving a hand to indicate Zuzanna, who is struggling in beneath the weight of a large carrier bag.

"I am *not* your assistant, Chloe. I'm only carrying this because you left it on the doorstep and I nearly tripped over it," she says.

"What's in there?" I ask.

"Quite a lot of elephants, judging by the weight," Zuzanna says, dumping the bag on the sofa.

"A big job requires big tools," Chloe says. She spots Lena standing looking uncomfortable in the corner and sticks out her hand. "Hi. Chloe Clarke. Fashion consultant and personal stylist." She must have been practising. "You're Lena, right?"

"Yeees," Lena says, shaking Chloe's hand and looking a bit scared.

I jump in quickly before Chloe starts the air-kissing thing and frightens her off completely. "Lena would like a new look," I say, "for the disco. Wouldn't you, Lena?"

"I'm, er ... not sure," Lena says, looking at the carrier bag and biting her lip.

"So I am willing to give up my restyling session

so you can help Lena out instead," I say to Chloe, trying to look disappointed.

"That's fine," Chloe says. "I'm sure we can do something with you, Lena."

Lena looks at me a little desperately, but I nod in a reassuring way.

"No need for you to lose out, though," Chloe says to me. "I can do you both. Double restyling. Introductory offer."

"No! I mean, there's no real need ..." I say, but Chloe is heading for the stairs.

"Bring the bag, Zuzanna," she calls over her shoulder. "We've got work to do."

Upstairs, Zuzanna is very impressed with my newly decorated room.

"Last time I was in here it was mostly a disaster, and now it's really nice. I love the colour of the walls."

"Thanks. My mum and Uncle Clive did it as a surprise."

"It's still small, though, isn't it?" Chloe says. "And no TV. I don't really see the point of a bedroom without a TV."

"Er, sleeping?" I say.

"Sleep? Oh, I don't have the time for that, darling. The fashion world is on the go twenty-four seven. Busy, busy, busy! OK, let's get to work." She takes the bag from Zuzanna and tips it out on my bed.

There are lots of scary hair tools, pots of cream and make-up, and multi-coloured nail varnishes. There are also lots of necklaces and ribbons, and a load of different coloured scarves.

"What are all these scarves for?" I ask. "We can't wear this many."

"Scarves? Don't be silly, darling." Chloe laughs. "They're my professional colour swatches. Expensive, of course, but a vital tool in the fashion consultant's toolkit. The first thing we need to do is find which colours suit you."

"But that's the scarf you wore to school today," I say, pointing at a purple one. "And you had that one on last week." I point to another.

"Do you want your colours done or not?" Chloe snaps. "Now, you and Lena sit on the bed. I'm going to drape the *colour swatches* over your shoulder and we will see which ones compliment your skin tone."

I sit down and Chloe puts a blue scarf around my shoulders. "That's nice," I say.

"Eeeurgh. Dreadful," Chloe says, and whips it off. "Makes you look like you have a skin disease."

"Does it?" I say, and try to look in the mirror on my dressing table.

"No mirrors!" Chloe says, throwing a scarf, I

mean a colour swatch, over it. "Not till the end when we do the *big reveal.*" Next, she wraps a piece of pink fabric round my neck and says, "Oh, no. So washed out." Then she tries a yellow, but that doesn't do either – neither does the red scarf, nor the purple one.

"Really, Emily, you have the strangest skin tone," she says. "Then again, I always knew this makeover would be a challenge." She drapes another scarf around my shoulders and suddenly cries, "Ah! That's it! It's totally you, darling!"

"But that's an awful colour," I say, looking at the luminous orange scarf wrapped around my neck. "I look like a traffic cone."

"It brings out the tones in your hair," Chloe says, turning to Lena, who is looking understandably nervous. "Now, let's start with you. Where's the red ... Ewwww! Not good. Shows up the red in your eyes. Perhaps you should get more sleep."

Lena's eyes are still a bit red from crying earlier. Her cheeks start getting red, too.

"Let's try this," Chloe says, wrapping a pastel pink scarf around her shoulders. She steps back and claps her hands. "That's perfect! You should totally wear pink."

"But I haven't got anything pink," Lena says. "I usually wear black."

"Pink is the new black, darling," Chloe says, moving towards my wardrobe. "OK, clothes. Have you got anything orange, Emily?"

"I don't think so. I was going to wear my blue dream-catcher T-shirt and leggings," I say.

"*Blue?* Do you want to make a total fashion faux pas? Now, let's see." She opens the wardrobe door. "Er … you don't appear to have any clothes," she says. "The rail's empty."

"But my dad fixed it," I say, looking over.

Unfortunately my dad's fixing seems to have come unfixed again. "Oh, they've sort of slid off."

"It's very disorganised," Zuzanna says, as she and Chloe rummage around in the clothes that have fallen to the bottom of the wardrobe. She does a 3.6 frown.

FROWN SCALE

Chloe comes up for air. "Your clothes are all totally the wrong colour, Emily. No wonder you always look so uncoordinated."

"There's a pink dress here," Zuzanna says, from inside the wardrobe. She pulls out Gran's recent purchase.

"I'm not wearing that, it's too small."

"It's not for you – pink makes your skin look like an old dishcloth. It's for Lena," Chloe says.

"Really?" Lena says, taking the dress. "It's not my usual sort of thing at all."

"Exactly. We are trying to give you a new look, remember."

"Nothing orange in here, though," Zuzanna says.

Chloe sighs. "Never mind, we'll just have to accessorise madly at the end. So, moving on. Hair," Chloe says. She looks at me and purses her lips. First she shoves all my hair to one side, then the other, then pushes it all in my face.

"Ufff," I say, pushing it back. "I can't see."

"You know, what you need is a fringe," she says. "Got any scissors?"

"No! You are not cutting my hair – no way."

"Don't be a baby, Emily, it won't hurt."

"It will. Every time I look in the mirror. You're not qualified."

"I saw a video on YouTube. It's easy."

"No. Never. Not happening."

Chloe sighs. "It *is* hard when you have to work with a difficult client." She turns to Lena. "Now, *you* should definitely have curls."

"Curls?" say Lena. "I've never had curls before."

"Trust me," Chloe says. "Zuzanna, can you start on Lena's hair? I'm thinking romance, princesses, er ... curly fries. Are you getting the picture?"

Zuzanna sets to work on Lena's hair, twisting long strands around the curling wand, while Chloe wanders up and down looking at me and making thinking sounds. "Hmm. Yes. No. Hmm ... got it!" she says, suddenly. "Eighties Retro. Why didn't I think of it before? Crimpers!"

"No need to swear," Zuzanna says.

"Crimpers for Emily's *hair*." Chloe pulls out a pair of tongs with wavy ridges on the plates. "They give you lots of little mini waves. Totally 1980s."

"But that was, like, over thirty years ago! How is that fashionable?" I say, as she starts combing out my hair.

"It's retro. Like vintage but newer. Try to keep up."

Chloe starts crimping

my hair while I try to work out how you know if something is vintage, retro, old-fashioned or just plain out-of-fashion. There must be a rule, but I don't know what it is.

Trouble is, I'm not sure that Chloe does, either.

"Nearly done," Chloe says. "You have very awkward hair, you know." She selects another strand and squeezes it tightly.

"Oww! You keep burning my ear!"

"First rule of fashion," Chloe says.

"What? Burn your ears?"

"No gain without pain, Emily."

"Finished," Zuzanna says.

Lena's hair is falling in lots of bouncy ringlets.

"Fabulous," Chloe says, "even if I do say so myself."

"Zuzanna did it," I say.

"Zuzanna is my assistant, Emily. She learned everything she knows from me."

"I did not," Zuzanna says. "I've only been your assistant for half an hour."

"I know. I'm a great teacher," Chloe says. "OK. You're done too, Emily."

She pulls my hair one last time, then nearly chokes me with hairspray. Then she steps back to have a look. "Hmm. Not bad, given what I had to work with," she says.

I'd have preferred "Fabulous!"

Next is the bit I've been dreading most: make-up. I have seen Chloe's attempts at make-up before: she doesn't get it in the right places even on her own face.

Luckily for Lena, she says, "We're going *au naturel* with you, Lena. A very light touch. In fact, it's more a case of getting that stuff off your eyes, rather than putting more on." She gives Zuzanna a load of cotton wool and the job of eyeliner removal, and moves on to me. "What we really need to do is draw attention away from your odd skin tone and awkward hair," she says. "Let's go brights! Shut your eyes."

With my eyes shut I can't see what colour the eyeshadow Chloe is applying is, but I have a very bad feeling about "brights".

"Great. Now just a smidgen of lipstick …" she says.

I open my eyes to see Zuzanna looking at me in a rather concerned way, but she quickly turns away and carries on painting Lena's nails pink.

"And we're done," Chloe says. "Hang on, nearly forgot. The first rule of fashion—"

"What, not more ear-burning?" I say.

"No. *Accessorise, accessorise, accessorise!*" Chloe says. She rummages about in her toolkit and says, "Perfect. Lena, this is so you." She fixes a pale pink flower in Lena's hair and then goes back to her rummaging. "Oh, yes. I think this works for you, Emily," she continues, poking something onto my head. "That's it. Finished."

She steps back and looks from Lena to me. "I am an artist, really," she says. "OK. I think it's time for the big reveal. Lena, do you want to come up first?"

Lena stands up. She actually looks really nice, with lots of dark ringlets falling around her shoulders, and the pink flower in her hair. And with no make-up, apart from just a little bit of lip gloss, you can see how pretty she really is. She holds the pink dress up in front of her and steps towards the dressing table.

"What do you think?" Chloe says, pulling the cover off the mirror.

Lena looks at herself closely. She twirls around a bit. "Wow. I don't look a bit like me any more. I look kind of … girlie," she says.

Chloe beams. "Totally de-emo-ed!" she says, covering up the mirror again. "And now you, Emily."

I stand in front of the mirror as Chloe pulls off the scarf for the second time.

I stare at my reflection.

I wasn't expecting "good" but I was hoping for a bit better than "totally awful". My hair is like a frizzy halo, sticking out all round my head, with an orange ribbon tied on top. I have matching orange lipstick and bright purple eyeshadow.

"I ... I don't know what to say," I gasp.

"Great, isn't it? So Eighties Retro. Loud colours are really on trend."

Unfortunately, they are also on me.

"I'm still not sure orange is really me."

"Of course it is, Emily. Isn't it, Zuzanna?"

"It's an interesting look," Zuzanna says, uncertainly.

"And my hair is—" I reach up to touch it. It feels sort of ... *crispy.*

"—amazing, I know! Although it would have been better with a fringe."

There is a tap on the door and my mum sticks her head around it. "Having fun, girls?" she says. "Oh my word, Emily, have you escaped from a Bananarama video?" she asks, laughing.

"A what?" I ask weakly.

"Never mind." She giggles. "Chloe, your mum's here to pick you and Zuzanna up."

"Five o'clock already! Time flies when you're being a creative genius. Pack the stuff up, Zuzanna," Chloe says. "See you at seven, girls."

Chloe and Zuzanna leave, and I go into my mum's room and come back with her hair straighteners and make-up remover pads.

"Chloe's not going to like it," I say, wiping off the purple eyeshadow, "but I don't think Eighties Retro is really for me."

Lena giggles. "I've seen sheep with better hair-dos."

"You look nice, though," I say.

"Do I? It feels so weird." Lena frowns. "Do you really think people will like me more now?"

"Well, you do look a lot less … you know … scary."

"Yeah. I suppose so." She looks at herself in the mirror again. "I'd better go and get changed, then. My mum said she'd give us a lift, so come round at quarter to seven."

Lena leaves me to find my way out of the eighties.

Once I have got the make-up off and sorted out my hair, and changed into my dream-catcher top and leggings, I feel a lot better. Then I remember that I still have to go to the disco and that I will never be able to hold my head up in public after it, and I start to worry again.

Luckily, it's about time to chat to Bella.

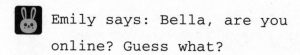

Emily says: Bella, are you online? Guess what?

Bella says: You've decided to go to the disco.

Emily says: That's amazing.
How did you know?

Bella says: Because I knew you'd
feel sorry for your dad.

Emily says: Well, guess what
else?

Bella says: You've made friends
with the weird girl.

Emily says: But how did you
know *that*?!

Bella says: I just knew you
would, once you stopped fussing
about how she looks.

Emily says: But that's just
it. She's changed. She's got a
new look. Normal.

Bella says: That was quick.

 Emily says: Chloe did it really, but at least Lena's not weird any more. I told her that she needed to fit in if she wants to make friends.

 Bella says: Or she could just be friends with the ones who don't care about what she wears.

I don't really understand what Bella is talking about. Lena looks really nice with her pink dress, and ringlets and flowers in her hair. What's wrong with that? She's going to be totally popular at the disco. No one wanted to be friends with her when she was Lena Lizard Girl, did they?

It's time to get going. I say goodbye to Mum and

Clover and go round to Lena's – by the front door, for the first time. Wanda lets me in. She is wearing a long black dress and has her dark hair loose.

I'm still not 100 per cent sure she's not a *you-know-what.*

 "Lena's still upstairs," she says. "Why don't you go up?"

I go upstairs and tap on Lena's door. "Hi, are you ready?"

Lena is standing in the pink dress, staring at herself in the mirror. "Yeah, I'm ready."

I don't know what it is but she doesn't look so pretty any more. Her hair is the same, she still has the flower at the side, but somehow she doesn't seem to look the same. And then I realise what it is.

She isn't smiling.

"What's wrong?" I ask.

She touches the ringlets in her hair and sighs. "I just don't think I can go out like this."

"But you look great. You know, fashionable and ..." *not weird*, I think.

"I just don't feel like me," she says.

And I think of how it felt to be in Chloe's Eighties Retro style, looking in the mirror and seeing the wrong person, and suddenly I realise what it was that Bella was trying to say. The person in the pink dress isn't really Lena – it's someone trying to be someone they're not. Lena will never really be that sort of girl. Lena is weird. She likes black, she likes reading at breaktimes, she likes stuffed crows ... and what's wrong with that? Perhaps being weird is OK. It was me who wanted her to look normal so I could be her friend, instead of being friends with the real Lena.

"Come on. We've got time. Where's your fishnet-sleeve dress?"

CHAPTER 17

Panic at the Disco

Friday evening

Lena is sitting next to me in the back of her mum's car with the black dress on and a black rose in her hair. We straightened out most of the curls but left some for fun. She has got her black lipstick and eyeliner on, too. She could look like the same old scary lizard girl but she doesn't.

She looks great because she's smiling again.

It's not till Lena's mum drops us off outside school and I see the queue that it all comes rushing back to me. Loads of kids in their best clothes all waiting excitedly to dance the night away. And, right next to them, in the school car park, a Leaks R Us van.

I feel sick.

"Emily," Zuzanna calls. "Over here."

I run over.

"What do you think?" she asks. She is wearing a short purple and white spotty dress with a matching headband.

"Cute. Do you know, I had a feeling you might have a new dress."

She laughs. "It's only from Tesco but I don't think that matters. I like it."

"It's Tesco-tastic," I say. "Where's Chloe?"

"Here!" Chloe says, running

up behind. "But … what have you done? Where's my Eighties Retro triumph?"

"Sorry, Chloe. I decided I like the uncoordinated me better."

"Oh, I give up," Chloe says. "Sometimes I think the world is not ready for my talents."

"I thought you were coming in your business suit, anyway," I say.

She is wearing a long flowery dress and a headband, and is also carrying a massive handbag.

"No, changed my mind. Business chic is *so* this afternoon. This is vintage, which is so now but looks so yesterday."

"What's with the big handbag?" Zuzanna says. "Is that vintage, too?"

"No, it was the only thing big enough to fit this in." She opens the bag and shows us a pack of coloured card. "Obviously, I only borrowed that card from school. It's not like I wasn't going to replace it."

"Come on," Zuzanna says. "Let's get in the queue."

"Hang on," I say. "Where's Lena?"

I look around, but Lena's not there. She must have thought I'd run off and left her. Oh no, I really have to find her – I don't want her to think no one likes her again. Just as she was doing so well.

Then I hear laughter from a group of girls further along the queue. A group of Year Five girls are standing together and they are laughing at Lena and I think, *Oh, no, poor Lena! It's my fault for making her come.*

I have to do something. "Back in a minute," I say, and go over to where the girls are standing. "Look," I say, "there's no need for—"

No ... hang on a minute. Lena is laughing too. They are all giggling together. She looks around and gives me a big grin. "Hi, Emily." She pulls me to one side. "The girls in my year have asked me to join them. You don't mind, do you?"

"Of course not. But how—?"

"I just decided to be brave and went over to say hello," Lena says.

"And it was OK?"

"A couple of them said they've been waiting to get a chance to chat to me, but they thought I preferred being on my own."

"Don't know where they got that idea." I laugh.

"Lena, come on, we're going in!" calls one of the girls.

"I was just wondering why your dad's van is here," Zuzanna says, when I get back to my bit of the queue.

"Oh, umm … he's just doing some emergency plumbing. You know – on that blocked toilet in the boy's cloakroom."

"Ewww!" Chloe says. "Who would ever want to be a plumber?"

"Look, there's your dad now," Zuzanna says. "Is that what he normally wears to work? And who's that weird-looking guy with him?"

"It's Mr Izzard, his assistant," I say, wearily.

"An assistant plumber in a purple velvet suit?" Chloe says. "I think I'd better give them my card."

The queue shuffles forward and we get closer to the door.

"Emily, cheer up. You look like you're going to the dentist," Zuzanna says.

"I wish," I say.

We join the excited crowd in the hall. The lights are still on – I suppose they will have to stay that way as I don't think Dad's attempt to make some disco lights out of a couple of torches and some coloured cellophane is really going to be enough.

Mr Meakin stands on the stage in his shirt and tie and jeans. He taps the microphone and says, "Testing, one, two, three … testing … Welcome to Juniper Road Primary's school disco!" Everyone cheers. "Now, I know you're all anxious for me to stop talking so you can get on and have a little *boogie*." He does a bit of a dancey wiggle and some of the Year Ones laugh. Well, two of them. "Tonight's disco is very special. Not only will we be having a disco but, later on, we will also be welcoming a very special live band on stage."

Everyone goes, "Whoooooo!" Everyone except me, that is. I make a sort of little choking noise and Zuzanna bangs me on the back.

"I would like to thank the PTA for all their efforts to make tonight's disco a success, and special thanks goes to Mr Sparkes and Mr Izzard for their very hard work."

"I wouldn't have thought unblocking a toilet was that difficult," Chloe says.

"Finally, I want to thank our super DJ who has kindly agreed to do the whole disco absolutely free and without payment, so that you wouldn't have to miss out. So, without further ado ... let's get dancing!"

This is it. If anyone was ever thinking of zapping me with a handy alien evaporation ray, now would be a good time.

Mr Meakin takes a step to the side and the stage curtains open to reveal ... DJ Derek Diamond's Disco! The main lights go off and the disco lights come up, and DJ Derek says, "Let's kick off with the NV Boyz!"

I can't believe it! Everyone starts dancing and laughing. I look again. It is definitely DJ Derek's disco, and not DJ Dad's disaster.

"Come on, Emily, dance!" Zuzanna says, pulling at my elbow.

I am just about to be ecstatically happy when I see Weird Griff moving some equipment onto the back of the stage behind DJ Derek and I remember – The Megatronics.

"Just going to the toilet," I say. I slip off down the corridor, wondering how long I can hide in there before someone comes to find me.

A couple of years would be good.

I am so deep in thought that I almost trip over the pack of coloured card on the floor outside Mrs Brace's office.

"Careful, Emily!" Dad is walking towards me with a bucket and his toolbox. "How's the disco? Better than my old vinyl, I suppose."

"Much better," I say. "I can't believe DJ Derek Diamond agreed to do it for free!"

"Well, not exactly for free – I had to go round and put a new shower in for him, and his van's broken down so we had to give him a lift to get here. But at least he didn't want any PTA cash."

 "You did all that ... just so we could have a disco?"

"Well, you didn't seem very keen on DJ Dad," he says, with a sigh.

"Thanks, Dad. It's brilliant," I say, and give him a hug. "Ewww ... what's that smell?"

"Oh, that ... I thought as I was here I may as well unblock that toilet they've been having trouble with." He holds out the bucket. "Found this old scarf stuffed down there."

"Ah. I think that might be Mr Meakin's."

"Perhaps it would be better if I didn't give it back."

"Yeees. I think he's getting a new one," I say. "Well done for the unblocking, though."

"I suppose I *am* a better plumber than a DJ. Although I was looking forward to being Disco Dad." He sighs again. "I really wanted to do my rap, and I'm sure your friends would have loved to hear 'Laser Love.'"

"I suppose they will soon," I say. "Live."

"How do you know about that? It's supposed to be a surprise."

"Don't worry, Dad," I say. "It will be."

My plan of hiding out in the toilet lasts about two minutes before Chloe and Zuzanna come looking for me.

"There you are, Emily," Zuzanna says. "You missed a whole NV Boyz song," she adds, managing to make it sound like a crime. They drag me back to the hall with them. There is no escape.

Lena catches my arm as I go back through the

doors. "Hey, Emily! School discos are pretty fun, aren't they?"

"Come on, Lena!" a Year Five girl says, tugging her elbow. "You have to watch Mr Meakin dancing – it's so funny."

Everyone cheers as Mr Meakin takes to the dance floor with Mrs Lovetofts. Mr Meakin has a special style of dancing: he sort of bends his knees and swings his arms back and forth so he looks like a soldier who's got his feet stuck in the mud. Mrs Lovetofts does this crazy, hippy dancing, waving her arms and swaying around. I think she might have got away with it at a 1970s rock festival, but she definitely needs to move on. It's like a sergeant major dancing with  a windmill. Everyone is giggling and laughing, and Alfie sneaks up behind Mrs Lovetofts and starts doing an impression of her, although I'm sure it's just an accident that she does a sudden windmill whirl and knocks him flying.

All too soon DJ Derek is saying, "Thank you and goodnight," and playing his last song. The curtains close and the lights go up and everyone groans as Mr Meakin appears on stage again.

"Thank you, DJ Derek Diamond. That was great. Next, we have a very special treat – our fantastic live band. This time I'd really like to once more thank Mr Sparkes, and in particular, Mr Izzard, who, being 'in the business' has been able to persuade such a great band to come and play for us. I hear they are ready backstage so, without further ado, I give you – the NV Boyz!"

There is a huge cheer.

"What? No!" I say.

Girls are screaming. So are boys.

Oh no, Mr Meakin has called out the wrong name again, just like at the fete.

"It's not them," I say frantically. "It's The Megatronics. He's made a mistake. You know he's not very good with names!" but no one can hear me above the screaming.

The curtains swish back to reveal four boys with floppy haircuts and tight trousers. That can't be The Megatronics. Maybe it's their grandsons? No, hang on ... it *can't* be ... live, on stage, in our school ...!

"Hello, Juniper Road! We are the NV Boyz!"

Everyone screams again. They burst into "The Only Girl", and everyone screams even louder.

Suddenly, I am very glad I didn't go to live in an igloo.

At the end of the song, Kit, the lead singer, flops his hair out of his eyes and says, "As some of you may know, this town is very special to us, as my nan grew up just around the corner, and I used to come here for holidays every year when I was young."

"Number 47, Cedar Road," says Zuzanna, with a sigh.

"And I also know that Year Six is making a donation to her retirement home. So we were really pleased to be asked to come and sing for you tonight. And I hope you'll all vote for us on *The X Factor!*" Everyone cheers madly again. "And here's another song you might know."

The NV Boyz play "Superstar" right there on the stage of our little school. I think it is my favourite song ever. Then they play "The Only Girl" again, and I think, *This is my favourite song, ever, too.* It is fantastic. There is so much energy – everyone is jumping up and down and singing along. Kit shouts out, "This school is fantastic!" and everyone cheers again. Then they have to play "The Only Girl" and "Superstar" again because they only have two songs from the show, but no one really minds. It's just too much fun to care.

After the third time round, Kit says, "We'd love to stay here all night, guys, but we have to get back."

"Boooooo!" we all say.

"Sorry this is such a flying visit but, before we go, we'd like to play one last song," he continues. "It's a cover of an old song and we're going to be playing it on the show next week. It's called 'Laser Love'!"

"Laser Love"! Oh *no*!

But, somehow, when the NV Boyz sing it, it doesn't sound anything like The Megatronics; in fact, it sounds quite good. OK, it sounds great! And, right, at the back of the stage, I spot Weird Griff playing his guitar and next to him my dad singing along. Well, at least he doesn't have a mop.

The NV Boyz sign loads of autographs before they leave. I think Zuzanna might faint when Kit brushes her hand as he signs a poster for her. She walks away holding her hand in front of her saying she'll never wash it again. Eventually, they leave in a coach and the whole school claps and cheers as they drive off down Juniper Road. Everyone agrees it was the best school disco ever.

"Wow, Lena! I can't believe your dad arranged that!" says a boy, who I recognise as one of the two who called her "lizard girl" in the playground earlier.

Lena smiles. "Yeah. He's pretty cool."

"They both are," I say, looking at my dad packing DJ Derek's Disco into the back of his van.

"But I still don't totally understand, Dad," I say.

I am squashed in the front of the Leaks R Us van with Weird Griff and Lena. We have just dropped off DJ Derek Diamond and all his kit back at his house, and now we are finally rumbling home. "How did we end up with the NV Boyz playing?"

"That's down to Griff," Dad says. "He knows everyone in music. He's even got us tickets to see The Megatronics next month."

"Luckily the same mate who manages The Megatronics knew someone at *The X Factor*, so he sorted out both things," Griff says. "Nice boys, those NV lads. Not my sort of music, but it's good to hear 'Laser Love' being appreciated by the youngsters."

"Yes," Dad says. "Not a patch on the original, though."

And he and Griff break into song.

"Yeah, baby, love you baby,

Yeah, baby, love you baby,

Yeah, baby, laser love,

Yeah, baby,

Yeeeeah!"

ACKNOWLEDGEMENTS

With thanks as ever to my wise and wonderful editor Kate, for knowing my characters better than I do and for listening to Chloe when she was crying out to be a Fashion Personal Stylist Consultant. Thanks also to Becca for patiently doing all the sensible bits and for being star baker and to Caitlin for never-ending Emily enthusiasm! To my family, friends and, ahem ... husband, for all their support and so, so many cups of tea. And, as always Gemma, President of Team Cooper, transcontinental superstar agent and my friend – thank you for being amazing at all of it.

ABOUT THE AUTHOR

Ruth Fitzgerald was born in Bridgend, South Wales. She grew up in a happy, big, noisy family with far too many brothers.

When she was six years old she wrote her first story, "Mitzi the Mole Gets Married", and *immediately* announced she wanted to be a writer. Her teacher *immediately* advised her that writing was a hobby and she needed to get a proper job. Since then she has tried twenty-three proper jobs but really the only thing she likes doing is writing.

Ruth lives in Suffolk with her family, one very small dog and five chickens. They are all very supportive of her writing, although the chickens don't say a lot.

Think it's a
happy ending
for **Emily Sparkes** ?

Think again . . .

For Emily Sparkes news, reviews

and totally awesome downloads

visit www.ruthfitzgerald.co.uk